AND THE HIPPOS
WERE BOILED IN THEIR TANKS

And the Hippos Were Boiled In Their Tanks

William S. Burroughs
and
Jack Kerouac

PENGUIN CLASSICS
an imprint of
PENGUIN BOOKS

PENGUIN CLASSICS

Published by the Penguin Group
Penguin Books Ltd, 80 Strand, London WC2R 0RL, England
Penguin Group (USA) Inc., 375 Hudson Street, New York, New York 10014, USA
Penguin Group (Canada), 90 Eglinton Avenue East, Suite 700, Toronto, Ontario, Canada M4P 2Y3
(a division of Pearson Penguin Canada Inc.)
Penguin Ireland, 25 St Stephen's Green, Dublin 2, Ireland (a division of Penguin Books Ltd)
Penguin Group (Australia), 250 Camberwell Road, Camberwell, Victoria 3124, Australia
(a division of Pearson Australia Group Pty Ltd)
Penguin Books India Pvt Ltd, 11 Community Centre, Panchsheel Park, New Delhi – 110 017, India
Penguin Group (NZ), 67 Apollo Drive, Rosedale, North Shore 0632, New Zealand
(a division of Pearson New Zealand Ltd)
Penguin Books (South Africa) (Pty) Ltd, 24 Sturdee Avenue,
Rosebank, Johannesburg 2196, South Africa

Penguin Books Ltd, Registered Offices: 80 Strand, London WC2R 0RL, England

www.penguin.com

First published in the United States of America by Grove Press, and imprint of Grove Atlantic 2008
First published in Great Britain in Penguin Classics 2008
1

Printed in Great Britain by Clays Ltd, St Ives plc

A CIP catalogue record for this book is available from the British Library

978-1-846-14164-5

www.greenpenguin.co.uk

Contents

AND THE HIPPOS WERE
BOILED IN THEIR TANKS

1945

by
William Lee
and John
Kerouac

Will Dennison
chapters written by

William Lee, Mike Ryko chapters

by John Kerouac

1

WILL DENNISON

THE BARS CLOSE AT THREE A.M. ON SATURDAY nights so I got home about 3:45 after eating breakfast at Riker's on the corner of Christopher Street and Seventh Avenue. I dropped the *News* and *Mirror* on the couch and peeled off my seersucker coat and dropped it on top of them. I was going straight to bed.

At this point, the buzzer rang. It's a loud buzzer that goes through you so I ran over quick to push the button and release the outside door. Then I took my coat off the couch and hung it over a chair so no one would sit on it, and I put the papers in a drawer. I wanted to be sure they would be there when I woke up in the morning. Then I went over and opened the door. I timed it just right so that they didn't get a chance to knock.

Four people came into the room. Now I'll tell you in a general way who these people were and what they looked like since the story is mostly about two of them.

Phillip Tourian is seventeen years old, half Turkish and half American. He has a choice of several names but prefers Tourian. His father goes under the name of Rogers. Curly black hair falls over his forehead, his skin is very pale, and he has green eyes. He was sitting down in the most comfortable chair with his leg over the arm before the others were all in the room.

This Phillip is the kind of boy literary fags write sonnets to, which start out, "O raven-haired Grecian lad . . ." He was wearing a pair of very dirty slacks and a khaki shirt with the sleeves rolled up showing hard muscular forearms.

Ramsay Allen is an impressive-looking gray-haired man of forty or so, tall and a little flabby. He looks like a down-at-the-heels actor, or someone who used to be somebody. Also he is a southerner and claims to be of a good family, like all southerners. He is a very intelligent guy but you wouldn't know it to see him now. He is so stuck on Phillip he is hovering over him like a shy vulture, with a foolish sloppy grin on his face.

Al is one of the best guys I know, and you couldn't find better company. And Phillip is all right too. But when they get together something happens, and they form a combination which gets on everybody's nerves.

Agnes O'Rourke has an ugly Irish face and close-cropped black hair, and she always wears pants. She is straightforward, manly, and reliable. Mike Ryko is a nineteen-year-old, red-haired Finn, a sort of merchant seaman dressed in dirty khaki.

Well, that's all there were, the four of them, and Agnes held up a bottle.

"Ah, Canadian Club," I said. "Come right in and sit down," which they all had anyway by this time, and I got out some cocktail glasses and everyone poured himself a straight shot. Agnes asked me for some water which I got for her.

Phillip had some philosophical idea he had evidently been developing in the course of the evening and now I was going to hear about it. He said, "I've figured out a whole philosophy on the idea of waste as evil and creation as good. So long as you are creating something it is good. The only sin is waste of your potentialities."

That sounded pretty silly to me so I said, "Well of course I'm just a befuddled bartender, but what about Lifebuoy soap ads, they're creations all right."

And he said, "Yeah, but you see, that's what you call wasteful creation. It's all dichotomized. Then there's creative waste, such as talking to you now."

So I said, "Yeah, but where are your criteria to tell waste from creation? Anybody can say that what he's doing is creation whereas what everybody else is doing is waste. The thing is so general, it don't mean a thing."

Well, that seemed to hit him right between the eyes. I guess he hadn't been getting much opposition. At any rate he dropped the philosophy and I was glad to see it go because such ideas belong in the "I don't want to hear about it" department as far as I'm concerned.

Phillip then asked me if I had any marijuana and I told him not much, but he insisted he wanted to smoke some, so I got it out of the desk drawer and we lit a cigarette and passed it around. It was very poor stuff and the one stick had no effect on anyone.

Ryko, who had been sitting on the couch all this time without saying anything, said, "I smoked six sticks in Port Arthur, Texas, and I don't remember a thing about Port Arthur, Texas."

I said, "Marijuana is very hard to get now, and I don't know where I'll get any more after this is gone," but Phillip grabbed up another cigarette and started smoking it. So I filled my glass with Canadian Club.

Right then it struck me as strange, since these guys never have any money, where this Canadian Club came from, so I asked them.

Al said, "Agnes lifted it out of a bar."

It seems Al and Agnes were standing at the end of the bar in the Pied Piper having a beer when Agnes suddenly said to Al, "Pick up your change and follow me. I've got a bottle of Canadian Club under my coat." Al followed her out, more scared than she was. He hadn't even seen her take it.

This took place earlier in the evening and the fifth was now about half gone. I congratulated Agnes and she smiled complacently.

"It was easy," she said. "I'm going to do it again."

Not when you're with me, I said to myself.

Then there was a lull in the conversation and I was too sleepy to say anything. There was some talk I didn't hear and then I looked up just in time to see Phillip bite a large piece of glass out of his cocktail glass and begin chewing it up, which made a noise you could hear across the room. Agnes and Ryko made faces like someone was scratching fingernails on a blackboard.

Phillip chewed up the glass fine and washed it down with Agnes's water. So then Al ate a piece too and I got him a glass of water to wash it down with. Agnes asked if I thought they would die, and I said no, there was no danger if you chewed it up fine, it was like eating a little sand. All this talk about people dying from ground glass was hooey.

Right then I got an idea for a gag, and I said, "I am neglecting my duties as a host. Is anyone hungry? I have something very special I just got today."

At this point Phillip and Al were picking stray pieces of glass out from between their teeth. Al had gone into the bathroom to look at his gums in the mirror, and they were bleeding.

"Yes," said Al from the bathroom.

Phillip said he'd worked up an appetite on the glass.

Al asked me if it was another package of food from my old lady and I said, "As a matter of fact, yes, something real good."

So I went into the closet and fooled around for a while and came out with a lot of old razor blades on a plate with a jar of mustard.

Phillip said, "You bastard, I'm really hungry," and I felt pretty good about it and said, "Some gag, hey?"

Ryko said, "I saw some guy eat razor blades in Chicago. Razor blades, glass, and light globes. He finally ate a porcelain plate."

By this time everyone was drunk except Agnes and me. Al was sitting at Phillip's feet looking up at him with a goofy expression on his face. I began to wish that everybody would go home.

Then Phillip got up, swaying a little bit, and said, "Let's go up on the roof."

And Al said, "All right," jumping up like he never heard such a wonderful suggestion.

I said, "No, don't. You'll wake up the landlady. There's nothing up there anyway."

Al said, "To hell with you, Dennison," sore that I should try to block an idea coming from Phillip.

So they lurched out the door and started up the stairs. The landlady and her family occupy the floor above me, and above them is the roof.

I sat down and poured myself some more Canadian Club. Agnes didn't want any more and said she was going home. Ryko was now dozing on the couch, so I poured the rest in my own glass, and Agnes got up to go.

I could hear some sort of commotion on the roof and then I heard some glass break in the street. We walked over to the window and Agnes said, "They must have thrown a glass down on the street."

This seemed logical to me, so I stuck my head out cautiously and there was a woman looking up and swearing. It was getting gray in the street.

"You crazy bastards," she was saying. "What you wanta do, kill somebody?"

Now I am firm believer in the counterattack, so I said, "Shut up. You're waking everybody up. Beat it or I'll call a cop," and I shut off the lights as though I had gotten up out of bed and gone back again.

After a few minutes she walked away still swearing, and I was swearing myself, only silently, as I remembered all the trouble those two had caused me in the past. I remembered how they had piled up my car in Newark and got me thrown out of a hotel in Washington when Phillip pissed out the window. And there was plenty more of the same. I mean Joe College stuff, about 1910 style. This happened whenever they were together. Alone, they were all right.

I turned on the lights and Agnes left. Everything was quiet on the roof.

"I hope they don't get the idea to jump off," I said, to myself, because Ryko was asleep. "Well they can roost up there all night if they want to. I'm going to bed."

I undressed and got into bed, leaving Ryko sleeping on the couch. It was about six o'clock.

2

MIKE RYKO

I left Dennison's place at six o'clock and started home to Washington Square. Down on the street it was chill and misty, and the sun was somewhere behind the East River piers. I walked east along Bleecker Street after going into Riker's to look for Phillip and Al.

When I got to Washington Square I was too sleepy to walk straight. I went up to Janie's apartment on the third floor, threw my clothes on a chair, and pushed her over and got into bed. The cat was running up and down the bed playing with the sheets.

When I woke up that Sunday afternoon it was quite warm, and the Philharmonic symphony was playing on the radio in the front room. I sat up and leaned over and saw Janie sitting on the couch with only a towel on and her hair all wet from a shower.

Phillip was sitting on the floor with only a towel on and a cigarette in his mouth, listening to the music, which was the Brahms's First.

"Hey," I said, "throw me a cigarette."

Janie walked over and said "Good morning" just like a sarcastic little girl and gave me a cigarette.

I said, "Jesus, it's hot."

And Janie said, "Get up and take a shower you bastard."

"What's the matter?"

"Don't what's the matter me. You smoked marijuana last night."

"It wasn't good stuff anyway," I said, and I went into the bathroom. The June sun was all over the room and when I turned on the cold jet it was like diving into a shady pond back in Pennsylvania on a summer afternoon.

After, I sat in the front room with a towel and a glass of cold orangeade, and I asked Phillip where he had gone last night with Ramsay Allen. He told me that after they had left Dennison's, they started out for the Empire State Building.

"Why the Empire State Building?" I asked.

"We were thinking of jumping off. I don't clearly remember."

"Jumping off, hey?" I said.

We talked along for a while about the New Vision, which Phillip was then in the process of trying to work out, and then when I had finished my orangeade I got up and went into the bedroom to put my pants on. I said I was hungry.

Janie and Phillip started dressing, and I went into the small alcove we called the library and thumbed through some things in the desk. In a slow sort of way I was getting ready to ship out again. I laid out a few things on top of the desk and then I went back into the front room and they were ready. We went down the stairs and out on the street.

"When are you shipping out again, Mike?" Phillip asked.

"Why," I said, "in a couple of weeks, I guess."

"The shit you are," Janie said.

"Well," Phillip said as we crossed the Square, "I've been thinking about shipping out myself. You know I have seaman's papers, but I never have shipped out. What would I have to do to get a ship?"

I gave him all the details briefly.

Phillip nodded in a satisfied way. "I'm going to do it," he said. "And is there any chance of our getting on the same boat?"

"Why yes," I said. "You suddenly decided all this? And what would your uncle say?"

"He'll be all for it. Glad to see me do a patriotic turn and all that. And glad to get rid of me for a while."

I expressed my satisfaction with the whole idea. I told Phil it was always best to ship out with a partner in case of trouble onboard ship with the other members of the crew. I told him that sometimes the lone wolf was liable to get the shit end of the stick, especially if he was one who liked to keep by himself all the time. That type of seaman, I told him, inadvertently aroused the suspicions of the other seamen.

We went into the Frying Pan on Eighth Street. Janie still had some money left from her last trust-fund check. She came from Denver, Colorado, but she hadn't been home in over a year. Her father, a wealthy old widower, lived in a swank hotel out there, and occasionally she got letters from him describing his good times.

Janie and I ordered plain fried eggs with bacon, but Phillip ordered two three-and-a-half-minute boiled eggs. There was a new waitress behind the counter and she gave him a sour look. A lot of people resented Phillip's exotic appearance and looked at him suspiciously as if they thought he might be a dope fiend or a fag.

"I don't want Allen to know about my shipping out," Phillip was saying. "The whole point of the idea is to get away from him. If he finds out, he's liable to gum up the works."

I laughed at this.

"You don't know Allen," Phillip said seriously. "He can do anything. I've known him too long."

I said, "If you want to get rid of the guy, just tell him to get off your tail and stay away."

"That wouldn't work. He just wouldn't stay away."

We drank our tomato juice in silence.

"I don't see your logic, Phil," I said. "It seems to me you don't mind his hanging around you too damned much, providing he doesn't make a pass at you. And he can be convenient sometimes."

"He's getting inconvenient," Phil said.

"What would happen if he found out you were shipping out?"

"Any number of things."

"What could he do if he found out only after you'd actually left overseas on a ship?"

"He'd probably be waiting for me at our foreign port, wearing a beret and cracking shells on the beach with five or six little Arab boys at his feet."

I laughed at this. "That's a good one," I said.

"You don't want to let that queer in on anything you do," Janie was telling Phillip.

"That's a good one about the beach, all right," I said.

Our eggs had now arrived, but Phillip's eggs were absolutely raw. He called the waitress over and said, "These eggs are raw." He illustrated the point by dipping his spoon into the eggs and pulling it out with a long streamer of raw white.

The waitress said, "You said soft-boiled eggs, didn't you? We can't be taking things back for you."

Phillip pushed the eggs across the counter. "Two four-minute eggs," he said. "Maybe that will simplify matters." Then he turned to me and started talking about the New Vision. The waitress snatched up the eggs and swished herself off to the slot where the food comes through from the kitchen: "Two in the water four minutes."

When the eggs came back they were all right. The waitress slammed them down in front of Phil. He began calmly eating the eggs.

"Okay," I said after I'd finished my breakfast. "Tomorrow you go down to Broadway like I told you and get yourself straightened out. I guarantee we can get a ship within the week. We'll be out on the open sea before Allen even finds out."

"Good," said Phillip. "I want to get out as soon as possible."

"There's no telling where our ship'll be going," I told him.

"I don't care, although I'd like France."

"So would I," I said, "but you've been to France."

"I was there with my mother when I was fourteen, with an English governess hanging around. The Latin Quarter's what I want to see."

"The Latin Quarter's in Paris," I said, "and all we have is a strip of the Normandy peninsula. I don't think we'll see Paris this time."

"There might be a breakthrough to Paris at any event. However, the main thing is to get out of America."

I said, "You're giving Ramsay Allen a broad berth."

"I hope so," he said.

"Lots of time to write poetry at sea," I added.

"That's another thing."

"Why can't you write poetry and work out your New Vision in New York?"

Phillip smiled. "Because Al's around, and he's a dead weight on all my ideas. I've got some new ideas. He belongs to an ancient generation."

"Ah," I said, "you betray a lack of gratitude for your old and venerable teacher."

Phillip gave me a sly undersmile.

Janie said, "Both of you are talking crap. You want to make some money, don't you? When you get back we can all go to Florida or New Orleans or someplace for the winter. Never mind the poetry."

We had cigarettes but no matches. Phil called out to the waitress, "I say, have you a match, miss?"

The waitress said, "No."

Phillip said, "Then get some," in his clear, calm tone.

The waitress got a wooden box of matches from under the counter and threw it at him. It lit in my empty egg plate and knocked some french fries out on the counter. Phillip picked up the box and lighted all our cigarettes. Then he threw the box back so it lit on the counter near her.

She jumped at the sound and said, "Oh! I shouldn't have given them to you."

Phillip smiled at her.

I said, "She must be having her period."

At this a short, stocky male waiter came up to me and said, "Are you a wise guy?"

"Sure," I said. It looked like there would be a fight.

Then Janie said, "That bitch started it all. Why don't you get yourself a new waitress?"

The waiter gave us all a dirty look and walked away.

"Let's get out of here," Janie said. She paid the check and we walked out.

We walked back to Washington Square and sat on a bench in the shade. I got tired of that so I sat down on the grass and started chewing a twig. I was thinking about the books I would bring for this trip and what a time Phil and I would have in some foreign port. Phil and Janie were talking about his girl Barbara Bennington—"Babs" to her friends—and what her reaction would be to this news of his sudden departure.

Then a little old man came staggering by, drunk and muttering to himself. He stopped in front of our bench and started staring at me. We paid him absolutely no attention, so he began to get sore. He had an alcoholic twitch and every time he twitched he snarled. He twitched and said "Aah" at me, and walked away.

Phil and Janie went on talking and suddenly the little drunkard was back staring at me.

"Who are you?" he wanted to know.

I twitched and said "Aah!"

"Go home," Phil told him, and the little drunkard got scared and went away, twitching and snarling at benches and trees.

We sat there awhile and then decided to go home. Phil said he was going straight home to start packing. He lived in a family hotel just around the corner from Janie's apartment, where he had a little two-room suite with private bath.

As we were turning the corner we met James Cathcart, a student at the NYU School of Business, and he went on with Phillip to help him with his packing.

Phillip was telling him to keep mum. Although Cathcart was a pretty good friend of his, Phil was taking every precaution in order that the news wouldn't leak out to Ramsay Allen.

Janie and I went upstairs and took a shower together. Then we sat down in the front room to talk. I was sitting on the rocking chair facing her and she was sitting on the couch with a towel on, native style. I kept staring at the towel and finally it began to annoy me, so I got up and pulled the towel off her and went back to the rocking chair.

She said, "What are you going to do out at sea?" and I said, "Don't worry about the future."

3

WILL DENNISON

I GOT UP SUNDAY AROUND TWO O'CLOCK, SWEPT UP the broken cocktail glasses, went down to the corner and ate breakfast and bought a *Racing Form*. I went back to my room and read the papers I had there. Then I looked through the *Racing Form* and didn't find any horses that I liked.

About four o'clock Danny Borman dropped in. Danny is a defense worker who looks like George Raft, except that he is tall.

It seemed things were not going well with him the past two weeks, because he couldn't get on a contracting job, where all the overtime is, and didn't want to tie himself down somewhere else. Finally he said, "Will, I'd like to ask a favor of you."

"Yeah," I said, "what?"

"I'd like to borrow your sap."

I'd been expecting a touch, so I said, "Sure, Danny, glad to oblige."

I went over to the bureau and fished my blackjack out from under a pile of shirts. I was thinking what a contrast this guy was to Phillip and Al, who will never lift a finger to get money for themselves so long as they can mooch off somebody else. I wiped it off carefully with a silk handkerchief and handed it to him.

"Watch yourself," I said.

He said, "You know me. I'm always careful."

He said he was going uptown and I said I'd walk out with him, since I was planning to drop in on Al.

At the door he said, "After you."

And I said, "Please, I am at home here," which I thought was pretty high tone, and he walked out first. Danny was a stickler for etiquette and knew Emily Post from cover to cover.

We rode up to 42nd Street together, and he got off there. I got off at 50th Street and walked over to Al's place, which was on 52nd Street between Fifth and Sixth, right over a nightclub.

Al had the best room in the house. It was on the second floor in back overlooking the yard. There was a picture over the fireplace, an underwater picture of a young guy in bathing trunks with a finger against his cheek, looking hammy and pensive, all done in mauve and light blue and pink. There was a long easy chair in the room, the only comfortable chair in the whole house.

There were two people sitting in the long chair and four people sitting on the bed, so I walked over to the high window overlooking the yard and started talking to Hugh Maddox.

Agnes O'Rourke was there, and Della. Agnes was sitting in the easy chair and Della was sitting on the arm of the chair. Della is an experienced lesbian at twenty, with two or three soul-searing affairs behind her and four suicide attempts.

On the bed were Jane Bole and Tom Sullivan. These two live together somewhere in the East Forties and make a round of visits every afternoon. Al was trying to get himself off their route.

Al was also sitting on the bed with Bunny, a girl from a good Boston family who says she is a kleptomaniac. Bunny was very much in love with Al.

Chris Rivers, who never takes a bath nor brushes his teeth nor cleans out his room, was sitting in a straight chair showing his teeth covered in green scum with a silly grin as he looked from one person to another.

I asked Hugh what was new and he said the FBI was looking for him.

"Yeah?" I said. "What for?"

"It must be about the draft. That's the only thing I can think of. They were asking about me down at Pier 32. Nobody knows my address down there."

"Well what is your draft status?"

"I don't know exactly. You see, I gave them an address care of somebody else and this girl moved after that, and when they came to my new address the janitor thought that they were from the finance company and told them he never heard of me. Then I moved out of that place without leaving a forwarding address because I owed a month's rent."

"What was your original classification?"

"It was 3-A, but my wife and I are divorced since then. That's two years ago."

Hugh is a longshoreman, about thirty, and Irish. He has one of the small rooms on the top floor next to Rivers. He comes from a rich family but doesn't keep in touch with them anymore.

"Well what are you going to do?"

"I'm going down and see them. No use trying to get away from those guys. I may get three years out of this."

"Oh just explain to them it's all a mistake."

"It's not so simple as that. Jesus, I don't know what the fuck's going to happen."

"What you need is a lawyer."

"Yeah, and pay him with what?"

The conversation was taking a turn I didn't quite like.

Someone stood up and said he had to go. Al jumped up and said, "Well if you must," and everybody laughed. Jane Bole dragged Tom Sullivan to his feet and said, "Come along dear."

They all left except Hugh, Bunny sulking because Al hadn't asked her to stay.

On the way out, Chris Rivers sidled up to me and borrowed a quarter. He could never work himself up to ask anyone for more than fifty cents.

Hugh stayed about ten minutes, looking gloomy and rehashing his problem.

Al said, "Well I guess it will turn out all right."

Hugh said he didn't know what the fuck was going to happen. "And don't say anything about this to Mrs. Frascati. I owe her a month's rent." Then he left to keep a date with his girlfriend.

"Thank God," said Al. "A little peace at last. Why, those people woke me up at twelve o'clock and they've been here ever since."

I sat down in the easy chair and Al sat on the bed.

"Now I want to tell you about the amazing thing that happened last night."

"Yes," I said, rubbing my hands together.

"Well, when we got up on the roof, Phillip rushed over to the edge like he was going to jump off, and I got worried and yelled at him, but he stopped suddenly and dropped a glass down. I went over and stood on the edge with him and said 'What's the matter?' and started to put my arm around him. Then Phil turned around and kissed me very passionately, on the mouth, and dragged me down with him on the roof."

I said, "It looks like you're getting there, after four years. Well go on—what happened then?"

"He kissed me several times, then suddenly he pushed me away and got up."

So I said, "Yeah, well what happened then?"

"Well, then Phil said 'Let's jump off the roof together, shall we?' And I said 'What's the point in that?' and he said 'Don't you understand? After this we have to . . . it's the only thing left. Either that or go away.'"

So I asked Al, "What did he mean by that? Go away where?"

"I don't know. Anywhere, I guess."

"Well Al, you should have said at that point, 'Okay dearie, let's fly to Newark tonight.'"

Al was very serious about all this, although it seemed pretty ridiculous to me. I'd been hearing about it since I met him.

Al said, "Well, I didn't have money, for one thing."

I jumped up. "Oh you didn't have money, hey? Do you expect to have money sitting on your ass? Go to work in a shipyard. Hold up a store. Here you've been waiting four years for this opening, and now——"

"Well, I'm not sure I want to."

"You're not sure you want to what?"

"Go somewhere with him now. I'm afraid there would be a reaction and I wouldn't accomplish anything."

I went over to the fireplace and banged my hand on the mantelpiece.

"So you want to wait. Tomorrow and tomorrow and tomorrow—waiting till you're dead. Do you know what I think? I think this whole Phillip complex is like the Christian heaven, an illusion born of a need, floating around in some nebulous misty Platonic nowhere, always just around the corner like prosperity, but never *here* and *now*. You're afraid to go away with him, you're afraid to put it to a test because you know it won't work."

Al flinched and shut his eyes and said, "No, no, it's not true!"

I sat down in the chair and said, "But seriously, Al. If you did go somewhere you might succeed in making him. After all, that's what you've been after these four years."

"No, you don't understand at all. That isn't what I really want."

I jumped up again, sneering. "Oh, so this is a case of Platonic love, hey? Nothing so coarse as physical contact, hey?"

"No," said Al, "I do want to sleep with him. But I want his affection more than anything. And I want it to be permanent."

"God give me patience," I said. "Patience I need." I tore at my hair and a little tuft of it came out. I made a mental note to go to 28th Street and buy some Buno hair tonic. It's got Spanish fly in it and there's nothing like it to stop falling hair.

"Now listen," I said. "I'm going to say it again and I'm going to say it slow: Phillip isn't queer. He might sleep with you, which I doubt altogether, but anything permanent is impossible. Unless of course it's just friendship you want."

I walked over to the window and stood with my hands clasped behind me like a captain on the bridge of a battleship.

Al said, "I want him to love me."

I turned around and took a toothpick out of my shirt pocket and started digging at a cavity. "You're nuts," I said.

"I know he'll come around to my way of thinking in time," Al said.

I pointed my toothpick at his chest. "Get yourself some scratch and he'll come around tonight."

Al said, "No, that isn't the way I want it."

"What you want is impossible."

"I don't see why it should be."

I said, "Well of course he isn't influenced by money at all, you've noticed that, haven't you?"

"Well, he is, but he shouldn't be. I don't want to admit that he is."

I said, "Facts, man, it's time to face facts." I took on a bourgeois *père de famille* tone. "Why don't you make something of yourself, something he'd be proud of and look up to. Look at you, you look like a bum!"

He had on an English tweed suit looking like it had been slept in for years, a cheap Sixth Avenue shirt, and a frayed Sulka tie. He looked like a Bowery character.

I went on, "Now I have it from reliable sources that there is at the present time a tremendous shortage of drugs in this country owing to the war. Marijuana is selling for fifty cents a stick whereas before the war it was ten cents a stick. Why don't we cash in on this situation, get some seed, and start a marijuana farm?"

"Well," he said, "now, that sounds good to me."

"You can buy the seed in bird stores. We can sow it out in the country somewhere and come back in a couple of months and harvest our crop. Later on when we build up a bankroll, we can buy our own farm."

We talked over this idea for some time. Al said he would go down and get some seed next day.

We went out to eat at Hamburger Mary's and he started rehashing the Phillip question. What did it mean when Phillip said this and should he call him up tonight or just go downtown without calling, was Phillip really in love with Barbara and if so should he do anything to break it up. So I ate my food and said, yes, why not, no, go ahead, and stopped listening to him. Like I say, I'd heard all this for years.

After dinner I said good night and walked down to the bar where I worked as a bartender.

The place where I worked is called the Continental Café. It is open all the way across the front in summer, with doors that fold back. There are tables where you can sit and look at the sidewalk if you want to. There are several waitress / hostesses who will let you buy drinks for them. Inside is the usual chromium, red leather, and incandescent lights.

As I walked down the bar I noticed a fag, a couple of whores with two Broadway Sams, and the usual sprinkle of servicemen. Three plainclothes dicks were drinking scotch at the far end of the bar.

I took off my coat and transferred everything from it to my pants pocket. I found an apron with a long string so I could loop it around and tie it in front. Then I stepped behind the bar and said hello to Jimmy, the other bartender, who was already there.

These three dicks said "Hello, kid" when they saw me. They had Jimmy waiting on them hand and foot, asking for scotch and cigars and lemon peel in their drinks and more soda and more ice.

I went up to the other end of the bar and waited on two sailors. The jukebox was playing "You Always Hurt the One You Love," and one sailor said, "Hey Jack, how come that machine never plays what I want?"

"I don't know," I said. "People are always complaining about it."

I could hear the detectives at the other end of the bar handing Jimmy a lot of horseshit about how he was a swell guy and so was the boss a swell guy and he ought to treat the boss right. These three were always in the place, sopping up free drinks because the boss thought they would help him out in case of trouble.

One of the sailors asked me where all the women were in this town, and I said they were in Brooklyn, hundreds of them on every corner. Then I started to tell them how to get there and they were so dumb they didn't understand me, but they left anyway. I took their glasses off the bar and sloshed them through dirty water and they were washed.

At this point, a man came in who was about fifty years old and was dressed in slacks and a light-gray coat and gray hat. He looked like a man of some intelligence and wealth. His eyes were bloodshot and he had been drinking quite a bit, but he had himself under good control. He went down to the other end of the bar near the detectives and ordered scotch.

I was mopping up the bar when I heard an argument down at the other end of the bar. This guy in the gray suit was arguing with one of the waitresses, or rather he was kidding her, and she was getting mad about it.

Then one of the detectives went over and called the guy a prick and told him to get the hell out of the bar.

The guy said, "Who are you?"

One of the cops gave him a shove and a second cop gave him another shove, just like a relay team, until they had him behind the phone booth. Then they pinned him against the wall and began slugging him methodically. They must have hit him about thirty times and the guy didn't even raise his hands. His knees buckled, so they took him and threw him into a chair.

After a few seconds, the guy started to come to, and he raised his hands like a man pushing covers off his face. At that one of the cops scented danger and hit him again, knocking him off the chair onto the floor. Then the other two helped him up and dusted off his clothes and found his hat.

One of them said, "Jesus, who hit you, Mac?"

The man's eyes were glazed. He looked like a case of light concussion to me. He looked blankly at the detective who had helped him up and said, "Thank you."

The cop said, "Any time, Mac."

The cop with the hat put it on the guy's head. He grabbed him by the collar at the back and by the belt. Then he shoved him to the front of the bar and gave him a push which sent him across the sidewalk into a parked car. He bounced off the car and looked around with that glazed expression, then staggered off in the direction of Sixth Avenue.

The cop came back from the door laughing like a schoolboy. The other two cops were leaning against the end of the bar.

"Let's have another scotch, Jimmy," said the cop who had thrown the guy out. Everybody in the bar was laughing.

Jimmy took his time about getting the scotch. I

could see by his face he felt more like serving those bastards a Mickey.

About fifteen minutes later the guy in the gray suit came back with a cop. The three dicks were still sitting there, but he couldn't identify them. He just insisted to the cop that he had been beat up in this bar.

I saw one of the plainclothes men give the cop the high sign, and the cop said, "Well, what do you want me to do about it, mister? You say yourself the guy ain't here. Are you sure you've got the right place?"

"Yes, I'm perfectly sure. And if you won't do anything, I'll find someone that will."

He was calm and dignified in spite of the beating he'd taken. He was smoking a cigarette and did not touch his swollen jaw and lips, nor call attention to his injuries.

The cop said, "Well what do you want me to do? You've had too much to drink, mister. Why don't you go home and forget about it?"

The guy turned around and walked out.

The owner had come down from his apartment upstairs and the cops were telling him what had happened. He said, "You guys better not be here. That prick looks like he will cause some trouble."

So the three of them left, looking a little worried.

It wasn't long before the guy was back, with five plainclothes men. They took the license number of the joint, talked to the owner awhile, and left. After that there wasn't much business.

Just before closing time a bunch of sailors walked by the place and I heard one of them say, "Let's go in here and start a fight."

The boss jumped up and said, "Oh no you don't," and closed the door in their faces.

After Jimmy and I got the bar cleaned off and left for the night, we saw the sailors slugging each other outside. One of them was laid out on the sidewalk. Jimmy said, "Look at that," and then we walked toward Seventh Avenue.

Jimmy began talking about how the cops beat that guy up. "I been around a lot," he said, "and I done a lot of things, but I never got so callous I could stand around and enjoy seeing something like that. Those morons in the bar laugh and think it's funny until it happens to them.

"Now if it was *my* joint I'd tell those cops, 'Now listen, fellows, you made a mistake. There's plenty alleys around here, you don't have to beat somebody up in the joint.' And then, on top of everything else, they walk out of there and don't even leave a dime on the bar. If they were any sort of characters at all, they'd say 'Jimmy here's a dollar for you.'"

4

MIKE RYKO

MONDAY AFTERNOON I SPENT LOUNGING AROUND the apartment. I was more or less waiting for Phillip to get back from downtown, where he was getting his papers in order. I took showers, raided the icebox, sat on the fire escape with the cat on my lap, or just sat in the easy chair thinking that if Phillip made out all right we could go first thing in the morning to the National Maritime Union Hall and register to ship.

Barbara Bennington was spending the afternoon with Janie. She used to come to Janie's apartment between classes at the New School for Social Research, and sometimes she would sleep there instead of going home all the way to Manhasset in Long Island, when she had early classes the following day.

Apartment 32 was by way of being a meeting place for her and Phillip, as well as a general hangout for our friends. Janie did her best to keep the place neat, but too many people came in all hours of the day and night to lounge around and talk and sleep, so the place was always a mess. The floors were always cluttered with books, old shoes, clothing, pillows, empty bottles, and glasses, and the cat used to prowl through all this as in a jungle.

Barbara was a sort of society girl with long black hair, very pale complexion, and surly dark eyes. She looked a little like Hedy Lamarr. She was quite aware of it, and sometimes she would turn on a demure, faraway look when you talked directly to her.

There really wasn't much in common between Barbara and Janie, except that Phillip and I, as friends, were what you might call their men.

Janie, although she, too, originated from a good family, had more of the expansive West about her than Barbara. Janie was a tall and slender blonde who walked like a man, cursed like a man, and drank like a man. You could see that sometimes Barbara's occasional coyness got on Janie's nerves.

They were sitting in the front room talking about dresses or something, and I was in the kitchen cleaning out a dirty glass that had a dead cockroach in it so that I could pour some milk, when Phillip got in. I stepped out of the kitchen with the milk and a liverwurst sandwich and asked him how he'd made out.

"All set," he said. He was carrying a big blue sea bag full of clothes and books. He put down the sea bag and showed me his newly acquired papers: a Coast Guard pass, a War Shipping Administration waiver, and an NMU book. I asked him where he had gotten the money for the union book and he said his uncle had given it to him with full blessings.

"Good," I said, "we'll go to the Union Hall first thing in the morning and register."

Phillip sat on the couch beside Barbara and showed her his papers.

She said, "I didn't think you'd really do it."

"Poor Babsy," said Phillip. "She won't have anybody to douse Pernod on her little belly anymore." He started to kiss her.

"That's what you think," Janie put in. "Do you guys think you can walk out on us like this and expect us to wait on our asses? Do you think women are suckers?"

"You've got to be faithful to the boys out there," Phil said.

"Yeah?" said Janie, giving me a significant look.

I turned on the radio and stretched out on the floor with a pillow under my head.

"I'm moving out of Washington Hall," said Phillip. "Can I live here until I get a ship?"

"I don't care one way or the other," said Janie.

Phillip got up and threw his sea bag behind the couch.

At this point, James Cathcart walked in and dropped his books on a chair. A big hulking sixteen-year-old freshman who was always giving out with the Noël Coward dialogue, Cathcart looked like the Hollywood version of the languid drama critic.

He said, "Hello, kids," and then turned to Phillip and asked him if he was still thinking of going to sea.

"You're going to help me move my stuff to my uncle's," Phil said.

"Then you are!" said Cathcart.

"Remember what I told you about Ramsay Allen. None of you are to tell him about this."

We talked for a while about the possibility of Al's finding out and what he would do if he did, and so forth, and then the conversation gradually drifted to general things.

Finally, Phillip and Barbara were discussing his favorite subject, the ultimate society.

"All artists," he was saying. "The ultimate society has to be the completely artistic society. Each of these artist-citizens must, during the course of his lifetime, complete his own spiritual circle."

"What do you mean, spiritual circle?" Barbara wanted to know.

The radio was on to an afternoon soap opera, and a kindly old country doctor who had just helped a young couple out of a scrape was giving them advice about life, with an organ-music background. "The thing that you must learn," he was saying, "is that sometimes you have to do things in this life that you don't quite like to do, but you've got to do them all the same."

Phillip was explaining about his theory. "I mean the circle of one's spiritual life. You complete the cycle of experience, in an artistic sense, and by means of art, and that is your individual creative offering to the society."

"You know," reflected the country doctor, "I've been practicing here in Elmville for almost forty-five years now, and in all that time I've learned one thing about human beings."

"Just how is such a society to be attained?" Cathcart wanted to know.

"I don't know," Phillip said. "This is the pre-ultimate society. Don't ask me about the details."

"Human beings," said the country doctor, pausing to puff on his pipe, "are essentially good. Now wait"—and he interrupted the young and bitter hero of the story—"I know what you're going to say. But, son, I'm an old man. I've lived a lot more than you have. You're only starting out on the road of life, and you might listen to what I have to say. Maybe I'm just an old codger, but—"

"There are artists in the pre-ultimate society," Phillip said, "who are contemporary models of the ultimate artist-citizen. I guess that as more and more people become artists, the nearer is realized the ultimate artistic society."

"Well," said Barbara, "maybe the Atlantic Charter is the first step toward an ultimate society. And certainly Roosevelt and Churchill aren't artists."

"Sometimes," the country doctor said, "sometimes the going is tough. Life is bitter, you get discouraged, you can't go on . . . and then suddenly—"

"Well I don't know about Roosevelt and Churchill," said Phillip, "except that they represent the type that is going to work out the gory details of progress."

"Then suddenly," the country doctor said, "something happens! Things suddenly start to break in your favor, problems get solved, the hard bumps along the road of life become beds of roses for a while, and you realize—"

"The artistic man alone will find the New Vision," Phillip said. Then he added, "For Christ's sake turn that fucking thing off!"

I jumped up and clicked off the radio. That sort of

put an end to the discussion. Cathcart went into the bathroom and Phillip and Barbara began to neck on the couch.

"Flaming youth," I said, and went into the small library. Janie followed me and sat on the arm of the chair.

"Mickey," she said, "don't go."

"Oh take it easy. We'll be back in two months with loads of money."

"Mickey don't go."

"Baloney," I said.

She was almost ready to cry. I took her hand and bit one of her knuckles.

"When I get back," I said, "we'll go to Florida."

"I love you," she said.

"So do I."

"Why don't we ever get married?"

"We will some day."

"You bastard, you know you'll never get around to it."

"Sure we will. Remember that letter I wrote you from New Orleans?"

"You were just horny then," she said. "You didn't mean it."

"Nuts," I said.

I'd met her a year ago when I thought I was Doctor Faustus himself, and ever since then we'd been living together in New York when I wasn't out at sea. The reason why we'd never actually gotten married was money, and I was always beefing about how I hated to work, so there it hung.

We went back to the front room and Phil and Barbara were still necking. Phil was on top of her and you could see her bare thigh. I wondered what prevented them from ever copulating. Sometimes they would neck all night long on the couch without actually copulating, sometimes even in their underclothing. That sort of technical virginity was a pain in the neck.

Phillip got up and said, "Let's all move my stuff up to my uncle's."

I wasn't keen on going along until Phillip told me there'd be drinks after. His uncle would give him some more money. So we all got ready to go out, except Janie, who went into the bedroom to sulk.

I went over and kissed her on the hair. "Come with us," I said, but she didn't answer, and even the cat gave me a dirty look.

So Cathcart, Phillip, Barbara, and I went around the corner to Phil's hotel, Washington Hall. We picked up all his junk in his room and took it down the elevator in dribbles.

There was a picture of Phillip's father on the wall that said WANTED underneath. Right alongside it hung a masochist's whip which Phil tenderly laid away in a box along with the framed poster of his father. There were also paintings in reproduction, books, record albums, easels, a saber of some sort, pornographic pictures, and whole boxes of assorted junk that Phillip collected all the time.

We finally carted all that out on the sidewalk and Cathcart went down to the corner to hail a cab. He was the type that liked to hail cabs.

On our way uptown Barbara got to talking politics with me, and finally we were on the Negro question. Phillip was talking to Cathcart and only half-listening to us.

"I like the Negroes," I told her, "but maybe I'm prejudiced because I know so many of them."

"Well," said Barbara, "what would you say if your sister married a Negro?"

"What!" yelled Phillip, and he turned to look at Barbara as though he were seeing her for the first time and didn't like her.

The cab was at this point rolling by Carnegie Hall on 57th Street and a shiny black hearse was cruising alongside of us. Phillip, instead of saying anything further to Barbara, suddenly stuck his head out the window and yelled at the hearse driver, "Is he dead?"

The hearse driver was all decked out in formal dress, black homburg and all, but his face gave him away.

"Dead as a doornail," he yelled back, and swung the hearse between two cars and slipped just by the curb and went on down Seventh Avenue. His face and his driving were all hack driver.

We all laughed and then we were on Central Park South, which is where Phillip's uncle lived.

We lugged all the junk into the lobby of the swank apartment house and Phillip had the doorman pay the cab fare. I told Phillip I'd wait downstairs and they all went up. I wasn't dressed for the occasion, since I hadn't shaved for two days and all I had on was a pair of chino pants and a blue sweatshirt stained with whiskey.

I waited on the sidewalk. There was a long orange slant in the street and Central Park was all fragrant and cool and green-dark. I began to feel good because it was getting dusk, and because we would be getting a ship in a few days.

After five minutes they came down and we all hustled around the corner to a cocktail bar. Barbara and Cathcart sat side by side and ordered beer, and Phillip and I sat next to them, side by side, and ordered martinis.

We finished the martinis and ordered two more. It was a fashionable place on Seventh Avenue, and the bartender didn't seem to like the way Phillip and I were dressed.

Phillip started telling me about Gerald Heard's *The Third Morality*, about biological mutation, and finally about how the more forward-looking dinosaurs mutated into mammals while the bourgeois dinosaurs became extinct.

He had a third martini. He looked at me intently and took hold of my arm. "Look," he said. "You're a fish in a pond. It's drying up. You have to mutate into an amphibian, but someone keeps hanging on to you and telling you to stay in the pond, everything's going to be all right."

I asked him why he didn't take yoga in that case, and he said the sea was more to the point.

The bartender had the radio going. A news broadcaster was telling about a circus fire, and I heard him say, "And the hippos were boiled to death in their tanks." He gave these details with the unctuous relish characteristic of radio announcers.

Phillip turned to Barbara and said, "Could you go for some boiled hippo, Babsy?"

Barbara said, "I don't think that's funny."

Phillip said, "Well, let's eat anyway."

We left the bar and went over to the Automat on 57th Street and each had a little pot of baked beans with a strip of bacon on top. While we were eating, Phillip paid no attention to Barbara, and Cathcart had to keep her company.

Then we boarded the subway and went back downtown to Washington Square. Phillip was leaning against the door watching the darkness reel by.

Cathcart and Barbara were sitting down, and I could see her getting impatient with Phillip's attitude. Cathcart himself looked as though he didn't think it was good taste on Phillip's part.

We went back to Apartment 32 and picked up Janie. She wasn't sore at me anymore. So we all went down to the Minetta Tavern and ordered a round of Pernods.

All during this time Phillip kept making cracks at Barbara until finally Cathcart said, "What's the matter with you tonight?"

It was the first time I had seen Phillip act that way toward Barbara, and I figured that now he had Ramsay Allen out of the way, he no longer had to rely on her.

By three o'clock we were all loaded on Pernod.

5

WILL DENNISON

MONDAY MORNING I GOT A LETTER FROM A DETEC-
tive agency to report to work. I'd applied for the job
about a month ago and almost forgotten about it. Evidently they hadn't checked on my fingerprints and the
fake references I'd given them. So I went down and
accepted the job, and they handed me a batch of sum-
monses to get rid of.

I stopped off at Al's about six o'clock that night,
after spending all day running around town to serve a
summons on someone named Leo Levy, who is a very
elusive Jew. Give a New York Jew a few partners and
he will get himself so incorporated you will always end
up serving papers on the wrong party.

Al was depressed. It seems that he had called Phillip
earlier in the afternoon and Phillip had said, "I think it

would be better if you stayed away from here." Al asked what he meant and Phillip had said, "Better for me."

I said, "Did he seem serious about it?" and Al said, "Yes. It was all said in a very sulky tone."

"Well," I said, "let it ride awhile, why don't you."

I sat down in the easy chair.

At this point there was a knock on the door and Al said, "Who's there?" and Agnes O'Rourke stuck her head in the door. She came in and sat down on the bed next to Al. She said, "I think Hugh is being held by the FBI."

"Yeah?" I said. "He told me they were looking for him. He planned to go down there this morning and see them."

"I called the House of Detention this afternoon," Agnes said, "and they wouldn't admit that they were holding him. I'm sure he must be there, because we had arranged for him to contact me if he could."

"Did you ask if they were holding a Hugh Maddox?" I asked.

"They wouldn't admit that they were holding anybody by that name."

So I said, "Come to think of it, I never did know whether his name was Madix, Madox, or Maddox, or how many *d*'s are in it."

We talked on about that for a while until the same things had been repeated three or four times. Finally, Agnes got up and left.

Al came back to the Phillip question. He said this new development was obviously a reaction from the scene on the roof, and I said, "You should have clinched the deal right there."

To this, Al repeated the old stuff, that he wanted something permanent, and I didn't even bother to argue. I said, "Let's go eat," and we went to the Center Grille on Sixth Avenue.

I had two vermouth and sodas before I could think about food. Then I ordered cold lobster. Al sat there looking sad and ordered one beer and cold lobster. Finally he said, "I think I'll go down there tonight and climb into his room."

I spat out a lobster claw and looked at him. "Well," I said, "that's taking the bull by the horns."

But Al was serious. He said, "No I'm just going to go into his room while he's asleep and watch him for a while."

"And suppose he should wake up? He'll think it's some vampire hovering over him."

"Oh no," said Al in resigned tones, "he'll just tell me to get out. This has happened before."

"What do you do?" I asked. "Do you just stand there?"

"Yes," he said. "I just get as close to him as I can without waking him up, and stand there till dawn."

I told Al he'd probably be arrested for attempted burglary, or shot, more likely.

He said in the same resigned tones, "Well, I'll just have to take the chance. I've looked the place over. I can take the elevator to the top floor, then climb up on the roof by the fire escape and wait there until three or four o'clock. Then I climb down into his room. His room is on the top floor."

I told him, "Don't get into the wrong room and start hovering over some perfect stranger."

He said, "Well, I know which is his room."

We finished dinner and walked outside. We took the Independent down to Washington Square and said good night at the entrance, because we were going in opposite directions.

I walked up Bleecker Street and there were a lot of Italian boys playing baseball with a broomstick as a bat. I was thinking about Al's plan to climb in and look at Phillip. This reminded me of a daydream Al had told me about once, where he and Phillip were in an underground cavern. The cavern was lined in black velvet and there was just enough light so Al could see Phillip's face. They were stuck there forever.

When I got back to my apartment it was too early

to go to bed. I fooled around the room for a while, played a few games of solitaire, and decided to take morphine, which I hadn't done in several weeks.

So I assembled on top of the bureau a glass of water, an alcohol lamp, a tablespoon, a bottle of rubbing alcohol, and some absorbent cotton. I reached in the bureau drawer and took out a hypodermic and some morphine tablets in a vial labeled Benzedrine. I split one tablet in half with a knife blade, measured out water from the hypodermic into the spoon, and dropped one tablet and a half tablet into the water in the spoon.

I held the spoon over the alcohol lamp until the tablets were completely dissolved. I let the solution cool, then sucked it up into the hypodermic, fitted on the needle, and started looking around for a high vein on my arm. After a while I found one and the needle slid in, the blood came up, and I let it suck back in. Almost immediately, complete relaxation spread over me.

I put everything away, undressed, and went to bed.

I began thinking about the relationship between Phillip and Al, and the details which I had learned in the past two years pieced themselves together into a coherent narrative without conscious effort on my part.

The relationship between them went back some years, and since it was Al's main subject of conversation, I was acquainted with all the details. I had known

Al about two years, having met him in a bar where I was bartender at the time. Here is the story as I pieced it together from hundreds of conversations with Al.

Phillip's father was named Tourian and he was born of uncertain parentage in Istanbul. He was a slender man with very handsome features. There was something hard and dead and glassy about the eyes and upper part of his face, but he had a charming smile. He had a way of turning his body sideways when he walked through a crowd, in a movement that was aggressive and graceful at the same time.

Outgrowing the crudities of his early youth, he gradually established himself as a sort of underworld broker dealing in dope, women, and stolen goods on a wholesale basis. If someone had something to sell, he found a buyer and collected a commission from both ends. He let others take the risks. As Phillip put it, "The old man isn't a crook, he's a financier." His life was a network of complex transactions through which he moved, serene and purposeful.

Phillip's mother was an American of a good Boston family. After graduating from Smith, she was traveling in Europe when her lesbian tendencies temporarily gained the ascendance over her inhibitions, and she had an affair with an older woman in Paris. This affair plunged her into anxiety and conviction of sin. A typical modern Puritan, she was able to believe in sin without believing in God. In fact, she felt there was something soft and sinful about believing in God. She rejected such indulgence like an indecent proposal.

After a few months the affair broke up. She left Paris, resolved never again to fall into such practices. She moved on to Vienna, Budapest, and came finally to Istanbul.

Mr. Tourian picked her up in a café introducing himself as a Persian prince. He saw at once the advantage of an alliance with a woman of good family and unimpeachable respectability. She saw in him an escape from her sinful tendencies and breathed for a moment vicariously the clear air in which there are only facts—and anxiety, inhibitions, and neurosis dissolve. All the subtle intuitive power that in her was directed toward self-destruction and self-torture was here harnessed to self-advancement. She made an attempt to incorporate this vision of harmony evoked by Mr. Tourian.

But Mr. Tourian was serenely self-sufficient. He did not need her, and she turned away from him and descended on Phillip with all the weight of her twisted affections. She dragged him all over Europe with her on continual obsessive tours and kept telling him he must not be like his father, who was selfish and inconsiderate of her feelings.

Mr. Tourian accepted this state of things indifferently. He built a large house and started a legitimate business that prospered side by side with his other enterprises, which absorbed more and more of his time. Drugs, which he had used periodically for years to sharpen his senses and provide the stimulation necessary for long and irregular hours, were becoming a necessity. He was beginning to break up, but without the conflicts and disharmony that accompany a Western breakdown. His calm was becoming apathy. He began to forget appointments and spend whole days in homosexual dives and Turkish baths, stimulating himself with hashish. Sexuality slowly faded away into the regressive calm of morphine.

Al met Mrs. Tourian in Rumplemeyer's in Paris. The next day he had tea with her at the Ritz and met Phillip.

Al was thirty-five at the time. He came from a good Southern family. After his graduation from the University of Virginia he moved to New York, which offered wider scope to his sexual tendencies. He worked as an advertising copywriter, a publisher's reader, and often he didn't work at all.

Al had an older brother who was ambitious and a steady worker. This man was about to go to town with a paper mill of which he was part owner. So Al went back home and got a job in his brother's paper mill. He had excellent prospects of being a rich man in a few years.

Phillip was twelve at the time and very much flattered that an older man should take the trouble to see him constantly and take him to cinemas, amusement parks, and museums. Phillip's mother would no doubt have been suspicious, except that nothing concerned her anymore but her illnesses, which were gradually taking organic form under the compulsion of her strong will to die. She had heart trouble and essential hypertension.

Al had tea with her almost daily in Paris and kept suggesting that, after all, she should return to America, now that she was so ill. There she could get the best medical care, and if the worst should come, at least she would be in her own country. Here he looked piously at the ceiling.

When she confided in him that her husband was a dealer in dope and women, he said, "Great heavens!" and pressed her hand. "You are the bravest woman I have ever known."

Now, it happened that Mr. Tourian was also looking toward the new world. His deals were so extensive that the number of people with real or imaginary grudges against him was growing to unmanageable proportions. So he began dickering with an employee of the American consulate. Needless to say, he had no intention of going through the tedious steps prescribed by law for immigration to America.

The negotiations took longer than he had planned. While they were still in progress, Mrs. Tourian died in Istanbul. For seven days she lay in bed looking sullenly at the ceiling as though resenting the death she had cultivated for so many years. Like some people who cannot vomit despite horrible nausea, she lay there unable to die, resisting death as she had resisted life, frozen with resentment of process and change. Finally, as Phillip put it, "She sort of petrified."

Phillip arrived in New York with his father. Mr. Tourian had lost his grip. About a year after arriving in New York, he was caught negotiating the sale of twenty thousand grams of heroin. He drew five years in Atlanta and the fines left him flat broke.

A relative of Tourian, a Greek politician, took over the guardianship of the boy. Phillip stole a WANTED poster of his father from a post office, had it framed, and hung it in his room.

As soon as Phillip arrived in America, Al began to commute by plane from his home in the South. Weekends in New York started Thursday and ended Tuesday.

One day, Al told Phillip that he had quit his job.

Phillip said, "What did you do that for, you damned fool?"

Al said, "I wanted to spend all my time here in New York with you."

Phillip said, "That's silly. What are you going to do for money?"

I got up the next morning with a morphine hangover. I poured myself a large glass of cold milk, which is an antidote for morphine. Pretty soon I felt better and went down to the office to pick up my assignments for the day.

I happened to be in the midtown district around noon, so I stopped off at Al's and we had lunch together at Hamburger Mary's. Al told me what had happened the night before.

When Al arrived at Washington Hall to hover over Phillip's sleep, they wouldn't let him up on the fifth floor in the elevator because no one was home, which upset his plan to get up on the roof before the front door of the place was locked.

So he went over to Washington Square and slept on a bench until two-thirty. Then he went back and climbed over the fence into the courtyard in back of Washington Hall and jumped up to grab the fire escape. This made a loud creaking noise, and before Al had even started to go up, the colored elevator man stuck his head out of a window and said, "What are you doing there?"

Al said, "The elevators aren't running. I just want to see a friend of mine, so I thought I'd climb up here instead of bothering anybody. How about taking me up in the elevator?"

The elevator man said, "All right. Come in here," and he helped Al climb in through the window.

As soon as Al got through the window, the elevator man produced a length of steel pipe stuck in an equal length of rubber hose. He said, "You wait right here till I get Mr. Goldstein," and waved the pipe in Al's face.

Al said he'd wait, and the elevator man went to roust out Mr. Goldstein, the landlord.

Al could have run out of the place at this point, but he realized that if he did that, he wouldn't be able to come back. So he decided to wait and talk his way out of the situation when Goldstein got there.

Goldstein arrived a few minutes later, in a dirty blue-and-white bathrobe with egg and coffee stains all over the front of it, followed by Pat, the elevator man.

Al said, "You see, Mr. Goldstein—"

Goldstein stopped him with outstretched hands. "We'll do the talking around here," he said in an authoritative voice. "Watch him, Pat!"

Pat stood there rocking back and forth on his heels, slapping the steel pipe into the palm of his left hand, with a crafty gleam in his eye.

Al went on: "I just wanted to see someone I know in the house."

Goldstein had picked up the telephone and was holding it in a lordly manner. "Who do you know in the house?" he asked.

Al said he knew James Cathcart.

Goldstein said, "Well, we'll check on that right now." He stepped over and rang Cathcart's buzzer. After a considerable interval, Goldstein was talking over the phone in unctuous tones.

"Mr. Cathcart," he said, "there's someone down here who says he knows you. We want you to come down and identify him. Sorry to disturb you, but it's quite important."

After a while, Cathcart came down from the third floor wearing a silk bathrobe. Al started to get up.

"Just sit right there," said Goldstein, and turned to Cathcart. "Mr. Cathcart, do you know this man?"

"Yes," said Cathcart. "What's the trouble?"

"We found him climbing up the fire escape, and he claims he was on his way to see you."

"Certainly," said Cathcart calmly. "I did plan to see him tonight, but I didn't feel quite well and I went to bed. It's quite all right."

"Well," said Goldstein, "if you say so, Mr. Cathcart."

Al said to Cathcart, "Well, I'll come back tomorrow, James. Sorry I got you out of bed."

"Okay," said Cathcart. "See you tomorrow then. Now

I think I'll go back to bed," and with this he started back up the stairs.

Al got up as if to leave.

"Just a minute!" said Goldstein. "You don't seem to realize that this is a very serious matter. If it wasn't for Mr. Cathcart, you'd be on your way to the police station right now. In fact, it's really my duty to call the police."

"Well," Al said, "I'm sorry——"

"Oh you're *sorry*! Well, your being sorry doesn't make any difference. I happen to be responsible for the lives and property of everyone in this building. Do you know that it's against the law even for people that live in the building to climb on the fire escape?"

"No," said Al, "I didn't know that."

"So you didn't know that, and you pretend to be a man of intelligence."

Al hadn't pretended anything. "Of course, now that you mention it," Al said, in placating tones, "it does seem reasonable. I guess I just didn't think."

"It's about time you did some thinking, isn't it?" said Goldstein. "Here you've gotten Mr. Cathcart out of bed and myself out of bed——"

Al said, "I'm very sorry to have disturbed your sleep."

"Well, that's not the point! This is a criminal offense. Why, if I did the right thing, I'd call the police this very minute. Do you realize that?"

"Yes," Al said, "I appreciate it."

"Well! You appreciate it, do you? The only reason I *don't* call the police is because of Mr. Cathcart." Now Goldstein shook his head and sort of laughed. "Why, I don't understand this thing at all. If you were a college boy, it would be different, but you're a man of practically my age."

"I promise you," Al said, "that nothing of the sort will ever happen again."

"Well, I can promise you that if it does you'll certainly go to jail!" Goldstein shook his head again. "Now, since Mr. Cathcart says you're all right, I guess we'll let it go. I really should call the police."

Al made a move to leave.

"Just a minute," said Goldstein. "You don't seem to realize that Pat, here, my elevator man, risked his life tonight. He ought to have some say in this matter." Goldstein turned to the elevator man. "Well Patrick, what do you think we ought to do?"

"Well," said Pat, "I don't like to see anybody go to jail."

Goldstein turned to Al. "I think you owe Patrick an apology."

Al turned to Pat. "I'm sorry about this thing," he said.

Goldstein took over: "It's pretty easy to say you're sorry. I'm not going to stand here all night talking to you. I've lost enough sleep already, though I guess that doesn't mean anything to *you*. Last summer wasn't it, Patrick, that a thief climbed up the fire escape and stole twenty dollars from someone's room?"

"Yes sir, Mr. Goldstein, I think it was," Pat said.

"We'll forget about this," Goldstein went on. "I'm willing to let it go this one time."

Al said, "You're being very lenient and I thank you. Sorry for all the trouble I caused you."

"I think a lot of Mr. Cathcart," Goldstein replied, "and I'm only doing this for him, you understand."

"Yes, I understand," Al said, and he began to edge around the desk.

"All right, Pat," said Goldstein. "Let him go."

Pat stood aside. Al turned around and said good night. Goldstein stood and stared at him and didn't deign to answer. So Al turned and slinked out of the door and went back uptown to bed.

Next morning Al came back to Washington Hall and found out from the daytime elevator man that Phillip had moved out of the place and was planning to get a ship.

"I've got to stop it," Al said to me at lunch in Hamburger Mary's. "He was planning to ship out without my knowing anything about it."

I said, "Well, you've got papers, why don't you ship out too?"

"Well, maybe I will."

6

MIKE RYKO

TUESDAY MORNING WE ALL HAD HANGOVERS FROM the Pernod. Barbara went to her classes at nine o'clock and Janie and I slept until eleven o'clock, when Phil got up off the couch and woke us up. It was a warm muggy dog day.

Janie went into the kitchen and heated us some soup. Phillip took a new pair of chino pants and a khaki shirt out of his sea bag and put them on. We were both dressed the same, except that my clothes were older and dirtier.

"Look at this place," I said. "What the hell happened last night?"

Phil said, "Where's the cat?"

We started looking around for the cat and found it sleeping in an open bureau drawer.

After we'd finished our soup, I said to Janie, "We'll be back tonight."

She said, "You'd better" and went back to bed. Phillip and I left for the Union Hall.

The NMU hall is on West 17th Street, about a ten-minute walk from Washington Square. I bought a *P.M.* on the corner of 14th Street and Seventh Avenue and we stopped for a while on the sidewalk to pore over the military map of France.

"They'll break out of the Cherbourg pocket and take Paris," Phil said. "Caen and Saint-Lô are ready to fall."

"I hope you're right," I said, and we hurried along toward the hall. We were all excited because we were headed for the front.

When we got to 17th Street there were scores of seamen standing around outside the Union Hall, talking and eating ice cream that a Good Humor man was selling.

"First," I said, "let's go across here and refresh our throats."

We went across the street and went into the Anchor Bar and ordered two beers. The beer was good and cold.

"These are all seamen," I said to Phil. "They are the wildest characters in the world, at least they were when I first shipped out in 1942, and in those days they were mostly seadogs, boy, especially on the Boston waterfront."

There was one seaman who stood out from all the others because he had a big red beard and Christ-like eyes. He looked more like a Village type than a seaman.

Phillip kept looking at him, fascinated. He said, "That one looks like an artist." Then, getting impatient, he turned to me: "Hurry up and finish your beer. We've got to register."

So we went across the street and into the Union Hall. The foyer was all done up with murals, one of them showing a Negro seaman saving the life of a shipmate, and it showed his muscular brown arm cradling the pale white face. There was a bookstand where they sold books such as Woody Guthrie's *Bound for Glory* and Roi Ottley's *New World A-Coming*, and varied pamphlets of the left-wing type, and the *Daily Worker*, *P.M.*, and the union weekly, which is called *The Pilot*.

We showed the steward at the door our union books and went into the crowded shipping hall. It is a long, low, wide hall furnished with connecting folding chairs, and with Ping-Pong tables and magazine racks at the back of the hall.

At the front end of the hall there is a big board taking up the whole wall, upon which numbers and letters are posted giving information on the companies and names and types of ships, where they are docked or at anchor and for how long, how many and what kinds of jobs are needed, and the general lay of the shipping.

The hall was crowded with seamen, some in uniform, most of them in civilian clothes. The nationalities were a kaleidoscope of racial types ranging all the way from sleek, olive-skinned Puerto Ricans to blond Norwegians from Minnesota.

At the other end of the hall, near the magazine racks, there was a desk with a sign over it reading CIO POLITICAL ACTION COMMITTEE. Phillip and I went over and looked at the pamphlets and petitions on the desk.

The girl behind the desk encouraged us to sign one of the petitions, which was all about a current fight in the House and Senate over a new postwar bill. Phillip and I signed them "Arthur Rimbaud" and "Paul Verlaine," respectively.

Then we went and stood in front of the shipping board to look over the prospects. There wasn't much shipping, because no convoys had arrived recently, but we went over to the registration windows and waited in line to register anyway.

I had to do a lot of running around the offices in back because I was behind on my dues and had overstayed shore leave by a couple of months. A union official who sat at his desk with his hat on gave me a lecture and pointed out that I was behind in my dues, and who the hell did I think I was? I nodded my head and shook my head and looked down at the floor until finally he allowed me to register as a member in arrears. This was going to make it harder for me to get the same ship as Phillip.

Meanwhile, Phillip was all set and registered. I told him to wait a minute and went to the open job window, to see if there were any jobs laying over. This is the window you have to go to when you are behind in dues payments, and also when you have overstayed your leave or anything contrary to the war-emergency rules of the union. The jobs available at this window are the leftover jobs that other seamen have rejected. You can always get a coal boat down to Norfolk or an ore boat up to the Great Lakes.

I asked if there was anything going overseas, and the open job dispatcher said no.

I went back to Phillip and we sat down and picked up some newspapers. I didn't want to tell him about my difficulties until I had done a little thinking on the matter.

The main dispatcher was calling the jobs over the mike and he had a Trinidad accent that was beautiful to hear. He would say, "Barber Line Liberty on line eight. We need two ABs, two ordinaries, a fireman water tender, three wipers, and two messmen. This ship is going far, far away on a long, cold trip . . . you gotta bring your long underwear."

And later he'd say, "Here's a job for a second cook on an old-type freighter. Anybody who comes from Chile can go down home."

Or else he'd say, "Out-of-town job, ship's waitin' in Norfolk, need three oilers, company pays your railroad fare down to Norfolk, pay starts today . . . here's your chance to ride in a Pullman."

Finally the dispatcher called for a whole deck crew. Phillip took out his registration card and said, "Come on." I had to explain to him that my card wasn't any good for these jobs.

"She's goin' straight across," said the dispatcher over the mike.

"Did you hear that?" Phillip said. "Straight across. France!"

"I know," I said, "but I have to wait for an open job. If you want to get on the same ship as me, you'll have to take your job at the same window."

"That complicates matters," he said.

"Well," I said, "maybe I can get this 'member in arrears' rubbed off my card. I can do it myself with ink eradicator or perhaps beef with somebody tomorrow and try to get a new card. I'll figure something out."

Phillip began to look glum. "Can't you pay your dues?" he asked.

"It's for five months and I'm broke, you know that. But don't worry, we'll get a ship together. Just leave it to me."

"Allen's going to have plenty of time to find out," he said gloomily. "And maybe we'll not be able to get a ship together anyway."

"Don't worry for crissakes," I said, "we'll get a berth before the week is out. I know the ropes, I've shipped out five times."

I got up and went into the latrine and there I met a guy I'd shipped out with before. "Hello Chico," I said. He was a little Puerto Rican scullion. "Remember me on the trip to Liverpool on the *George Weems*?"

Chico grinned blankly. Chico had been out so many times he couldn't remember one trip from another, or maybe he just couldn't remember what happened from one minute to the other.

"Well, so long Chico," I said, buttoning my fly.

"So long," said Chico.

I went back into the hall. It was almost closing time. Phillip was sitting in the same chair.

A seaman came up to me and said, "Listen feller, give me a dime, will ya?" No questions asked I gave him a dime. This guy was going all over the hall collecting dimes. I figured he was one of the old-type seamen like I had seen on the Boston waterfront in 1942 and that he needed a few drinks. Most of these old seadogs had been torpedoed and drowned before the land war even started to get hot.

I looked around the hall at the new-type seamen. A lot of them wore uniforms and gold braid that they bought in army-navy stores. These were the characters who didn't drink much and spent all their time in seaman's clubs and canteens, playing society boys with the society girls and actresses that worked as hostesses. Then there were a large number of nondescript, rather shady-looking characters who probably had drifted into the merchant marine trailing their records behind them. Finally I noticed a third general group, a batch of youngsters from all over the country, reminiscent of the teenage sailors in the navy who you find sleeping in the subway with their mouths open and their legs spread all the way across the aisle.

The hall was beginning to empty out and now an old Swede was coming around with a broom. The dispatcher had gone home and the girl in front of the board with the earphones was gone home, and I guess Joe Curran was gone home too. It was thick and gray outside. Phillip and I sat in the empty row and smoked the last cigarette.

Suddenly Phil said, "If we go to France, let's jump ship and hike to Paris. I want to live in the Latin Quarter."

"What about the war?" I asked.

"Oh, it'll probably be over by the time we get there."

I gave this a thought for a while.

"Well," I said, "I wouldn't embark on anything like that unless I were drunk."

"We'll get drunk in port and start off in the middle of the night."

"What about MPs and French authorities and all that?"

"We'll worry about that when the time comes," he said.

"I'd do anything if I were drunk," I said.

We sat there thinking about this new plan, and the more I thought about it, the more I felt the dare, although somewhere in the back of my mind I knew it couldn't work and we'd be arrested.

Phillip lapsed into a sort of meditative silence so I started talking to him. "You'll like shipping out," I said. "Boy, when you get to port there's nothing like it."

"One time my ship got into a little port in Nova Scotia called Sydney. We'd been anchored in an Arctic Greenland fjord for two months and every one of us was all wound up for a big drunk. The whole crew went ashore—a hundred and fifty of us, it was a medium-sized transport cargo—and only fifty of us managed to stay out of jail. One of them was arrested for jacking off a horse on Main Street. Another was walking around with his dick dangling out because he'd forgotten to put it back in after taking a leak, so they pulled him in.

"I was walking along with a bunch of shipmates and we all went down to the waterfront and found a shack and started fooling around. Two of the guys went inside the shack and then one of them poked his head out of a hole in the roof and started singing. Some of the guys were pushing against the shack to see if it would move. It did. While the two seamen were still in the shack, we pushed it over the side right into the water. It's a wonder they didn't drown. Maybe they were too drunk to drown.

"Later, I was walking up an alley with a full quart of whiskey that a guy who had six of them stuck all over his pockets gave me, when I came on a shipmate of mine bending over a man's body. The man—he looked like a Sydney waterfront bum—was dead drunk and this shipmate was taking his wallet. 'Keep your fucking mouth shut about this,' he said to me, standing up with the wallet in his hand. 'It's your business, not mine,' I said. He laughed and asked for a drink, but I left because I didn't like him much.

"I was ashore for three days on a twelve-hour pass. On the third day, in the afternoon, I was walking with a guy in back of the Sydney YMCA when here comes two Canadian SPs and two army MPs from our own ship. They had guns and told us to come with them. My buddy started running up the alley and they shot over his head, so he came back, laughing. We were still drunk—we'd been drunk all the three days—and we didn't care about anything

"Anyway, the MPs and the SPs took this guy and I to a Canadian corvette base and had us put in the guardhouse until the Liberty boat was to come and pick us up and take us back to our ship. So we slept for a couple of hours. You wouldn't believe it, but I was so drunk and tired I slept on two sawhorses I put next to each other. I was drunk and I kept saying to myself that I mustn't sleep on the floor and get my clothes dirty. So here I lay in a little ball on top of two sawhorses and slept.

"Finally I woke up and it was getting dark. There were some British sailors playing catch with a ball and gloves outside the guardhouse. I jumped out the window at the side and walked around the guardhouse and started playing with them. They were awkward and didn't know how to throw, so I kept giving them the fancy Bob Feller windup. Then it got dark and the game broke up. There were no guards around, I guess they were eating chow, so I jumped over the fence surrounding the base and went back into town.

"I started drinking again. That night I went up to the suburbs of Sydney where no SPs would be likely to find me. This neighborhood consisted of miners who worked in the Princess Colliery. I drank in several little honky-tonk joints and finally picked up a De Soto Indian girl. I stayed most of the night in a windswept cottage with her until she kicked me out. I was sleepy now so I went into the first house I saw down the street and went to sleep on the couch.

"I kept convincing myself it was the back room of a honky-tonk joint. But when the sun came up, I found that there were two other guys from my ship sleeping on the floor and that we were in the front room of somebody's home because you could hear the family at the breakfast table in the kitchen down the hall. Finally the man of the house, a miner, came clumping down the hall with his lunch pail and then saw us in the parlor. He said, 'Good morning boys,' and went out. I never had seen anything to beat it, it was so crazy.

"We left the house and passed a store and the first thing I knew one of the jackoff seamen put his fist through the plate-glass window. We ran in all directions and finally I got back to town on a trolley and went into a bar. I had a few drinks and decided to get some sleep.

"None of us dared to go into the seaman's club because the MPs would surely keep a lookout there for us, but I decided to go anyway because I was tired and it was time to give myself up. Funny thing was, the MPs weren't there. Nobody was there, just a big hall full of empty cots, with everybody gone hiding or arresting one another. So I went to sleep on one of the cots and had a good long rest.

"I woke up refreshed and went downtown that night and got drunk again. I noticed I didn't have any money left, to speak of, so I boarded a Liberty boat and went back to my ship. That night, we pulled out with everybody accounted for, and I was one of the last of the stragglers. I was logged five bucks.

"We got to Boston three days later after a stopover in Halifax, and it started all over again. Here were these seamen with their thousand-dollar payoffs staggering drunkenly off the gangplank with all the things they'd picked up in Greenland: small kayaks, harpoons, fish spears, stinking furs, skins, everything. I had a harpoon. Me and a few other guys stashed all our stuff away in the baggage room of North Station and wired home most of our money. Then we started out on a binge.

"It was a Saturday night, I remember, and October. I drank at least forty-five or fifty glasses of beer that night, and that's no lie. We were down in South Boston taking over joint after joint and singing over microphones on bandstands and banging on drums and all that. Then we sort of drifted toward Scollay Square and wound up in that joint of joints, the Imperial Café. Here were two floors and five rooms of sailors, soldiers, and seamen, women, music, whiskey, smoke, and fights.

"It was all a blur to me. I remember later on we were standing in a courtyard somewhere in midtown Boston and the seaman with me was calling up to a second-story window where a whore was supposed to live. The window opened and this big Negro stuck his head out and poured a bucket of hot water down on us.

"Well, finally, the sun came up, and I was lying on a City Department toolbox on Atlantic Avenue, right on the waterfront, and there were all these little fishing smacks docked right beside me with the red sun touching their masts. I watched that for a while, then I sort of dragged myself to North Station to get my gear, and then had to go across town in a taxi to South Station and buy a ticket for New York. I'll never forget that glorious return to our fair shores."

Phillip was smiling all the way through my story. It was almost dark outside, so cloudy and gray it looked like a rainy dusk. The old Swede had finished his sweeping.

"Let's go to Dennison's," Phil said. "All this makes me want to get drunk and we haven't any money."

"Okay with me," I said and we started out of the hall.

We were on the steps and suddenly I saw a familiar figure coming down 17th Street toward the hall.

"Look who's coming," I said.

It was Ramsay Allen, and he hadn't seen us yet. He
was hurrying in long, eager strides, and the expression
on his face was like that of the mother of a lost child
rushing to the police station to find out if the child
they're holding there is hers. Then he saw us. His face
lit up instantly with recognition and joy, then the old
affable and sophisticated expression readjusted itself.

"Well," he said as he came up, "what's been going
on behind my back?" We all smiled as though we were
proud of our separate achievements. Then Al looked
seriously at Phillip: "You haven't got a ship, have you?"

"Not yet," said Phillip.

We started walking. Neither one of them said a
word about anything of much point. Phil started to tell
him about our new plan to jump ship in France and go
to Paris, and Al said, "Do you think it's safe?"

"We're not worried about that," Phil said.

We walked down to Dennison's place and sat on his
doorstep to wait for him to come home from work. We
waited awhile, and then we walked over to Chumley's,
where he generally eats.

7

WILL DENNISON

TUESDAY NIGHT I MET HELEN IN CHUMLEY'S. Helen was a hostess from the Continental Café. We had some vermouth and soda, and I drank the first one right down. I was so thirsty from running around all day, I felt like my mouth was going to jump right out at that vermouth like a Mexican drawing I saw once in a museum where a guy was represented with his mouth sticking out on the end of a long tube like it couldn't wait for the rest of his face. In the middle of the second vermouth I felt a little better and dropped my hand down on Helen's bare knee and squeezed it.

She said, "Why, Mr. Dennison!" and I gave her a paternal smile.

I looked up and saw a good-looking young man in merchant marine khaki come through the door. It was a fraction of a second before I realized it was Phillip. I looked right at him and didn't recognize him. Then I saw Al and Ryko behind him.

They came over to the table and we said hello all round. Then the waiter put two tables together and we moved over.

Phillip said, "Well Dennison, we're shipping out tomorrow. This may be the last time we'll ever see each other."

"So I hear."

Al said, "They plan to go to France and jump ship."

I turned to Phillip and said, "What are you going to do in France?"

He went into a long spiel. "When we get there we're going to jump ship and start off cross-country for Paris. By then the Allies will have broken through to Paris and maybe the war will be over. We're going to pose as Frenchmen. Since I can't speak French very fluently, I'm to be a sort of idiot peasant. Mike, who speaks good French, is going to do all the talking. We'll travel by oxcart and sleep in haylofts till we get to the Left Bank."

I listened to this for a while, then I said, "What are you going to do for food? Everything is rationed. You need books for everything."

He said, "Oh we'll just say we lost our books. We'll say we're refugees just back from a concentration camp."

"Who's going to say all this?"

"Ryko. He's half French. I'm going to be deaf and dumb."

I looked dubiously at Ryko and he said, "That's right. My mother taught me French. And I can speak Finnish too."

"Oh well," I said, "do what you like. It's no skin off me."

Then Al said, "I don't think it's a good idea at all."

I said, "Caution is no virtue in the young. In fact, come to think of it, it's a good idea."

Al gave me a furious look which I ignored.

"France . . ." I said dreamily. "Well, give my regards to the place when you gets there—*if* you gets there."

The food began to arrive at this point. First shrimps, then hot soup, which was put on the table at the same time as another round of cocktails. This is something that usually happens, and the result is that either the soup gets cold while you're drinking the cocktail or you drink the soup, which spoils the effect of the cocktail.

We finished dinner a while later and Helen said she was going home to Queens. Al gave me four dollars, which was supposed to pay for all the food and cocktails he and Ryko and Phillip had guzzled down, but I was glad to get even that much.

We went out in the street and walked around talking about what we were going to do. Al said, "Well, we might go and see Connie."

Phillip asked, "Who's Connie?"

"She's the girl that works on *P.M.*," Al answered. "The one I told you about I laid on the roof two weeks ago."

So Ryko said, "Okay, let's go."

Al said, "But the only trouble is she moved, and I haven't got her new address, or I lost it. I'd have to find out from Agnes or somebody."

"Well," I put in, "we can't go there then."

Al said, "No, I guess not."

At this point a black-haired boy of about twelve walked by, and Al said, "Hiya, Harry," and the boy said, "Hiya, Al."

There was a big crap game in front of Romany Marie's, several hundred dollars in the street. We stopped for a while to watch the game. A fat greasy character with a big cigar picked up the dice, throwing down five dollars. He rolled a ten. The gamblers stood around with money in their hands and money pinned under their feet to keep it from blowing away. They started laying bets with the shooter and side bets with each other.

"Four to two no ten."

"Five no ten eleven."

"Two no ten a three."

The shooter took about thirty dollars of the two-to-one bets. He hit the ten and collected money from all sides, gathering bills from under people's shoes and from outstretched hands. Leaving ten on the ground, he said, "Shoot it." Someone faded him. The come-out was a seven. He doubled again, shooting the twenty.

They were all taut and tense with purpose. The dice hit a board and bounced off, coming out a nine. The wrong bettors started laying the odds.

"Six to four no nine."

"Ten no nine a three."

"Five he's right on the come-out."

There was no small talk whatever.

We walked on. Al said, "We might go see Mary-Ann. She's pretty nice. Only trouble is, she's got that godawful husband, and they never serve any liquor."

Phillip said, "Let's go in George's and have a drink."

"How about Betty-Lou?" I put in.

"All right, let's go there."

We walked toward Betty-Lou's place, which is back the way we had come from, in irregular straggling groups.

On the way, Phillip jumped up and pulled a branch off a tree. Al looked at me and said, "Isn't he wonderful?"

Betty-Lou lived in a cellar apartment. She was a southern girl and a Christian Scientist who was in radio and felt strongly about the future educational mission of radio. It seems that after the war you won't be able to keep off all the culture that will be poured onto you out of radios because they're going to make recordings of university lectures on all subjects and play them twenty-four hours a day.

I told her it sounded awful to me, and she said I was "terribly cynical."

When we got there Betty-Lou had a visitor. He was a little man from Brooklyn who looked like a cabdriver. He wore a double-breasted suit and a loud tie in spite of the weather and was obviously on his best behavior. He had brought a bottle of California Burgundy and some sliced cold roast beef for Betty-Lou. Phillip greeted him in an offhand way and proceeded immediately to help himself to beef and wine. Al did the same and they both ignored the man from Brooklyn.

Ryko and I sat down and lapsed into a gloomy silence. Phillip was still eating roast beef with one hand while he began pulling books out of the case and turning the pages with his greasy fingers. I pulled myself together and asked Betty-Lou a few questions about radio.

After a few minutes the man from Brooklyn got up to leave. He shook hands with Ryko and me. He glanced uncertainly at Al and Phillip. Phillip was now shuffling through a stack of records and Al was sitting cross-legged on the floor looking up at him.

The man from Brooklyn said, "Well I gotta be getting along."

Betty-Lou walked to the door with him and told him to come again.

Phillip and Al were fooling with the phonograph and got it working, so they put on a record from *Swan Lake*.

Suddenly a large brown rat ran out of the kitchen and into the middle of the room. He stood there indecisively for a moment, then gave a squeak and ran into the bathroom.

Betty-Lou said, "Landsakes! There's that old rat again."

She went into the kitchen and buttered a graham cracker with phosphorus paste. She broke the cracker up and scattered pieces of it around the kitchen and in the bathroom. I knew this wouldn't do any good because rats get wise to phosphorus paste. And besides, there were so many holes in her apartment that all the rats in New York could come in.

Presently two men and a girl arrived, and I started a dull conversation with one of the men. We were talking about the bad quality of Cuban gin, and high prices of liquor generally. He said his favorite drink was scotch and I said mine was cognac, but you couldn't get it anymore. He said, "Yes, you can still get it."

I said, "Yes, at a dollar a shot." I took a deep breath and went on to say that cognac apparently couldn't be produced anywhere except in Cognac, France. "No brandy anywhere else tastes anything like it."

He considered this awhile and said, "California brandy is terrible."

I said, "I don't like Spanish brandy."

"Well," he said, "I don't care much for brandy."

There was a long silence. I excused myself and went to the toilet and leaned against the wall, keeping a sharp eye out for the rats.

When I returned, Al and Phillip were preparing to go out and buy a bottle of rum with money subscribed by the two men. I went over and began playing records to avoid conversation. Ryko was talking to Betty-Lou, and I could overhear that it was about Phillip. Ryko seemed to be making headway with her.

Al and Phillip finally came back with two French sailors they had picked up in George's. Everyone began to talk bad French, except the sailors who were talking bad English. They were trying to get across that they were respectable characters who were not used to taking up with strangers and everyone kept telling them that it was all right.

Finally, the party disbanded and we walked out onto the street. Phillip wanted something to eat, so we started up Seventh Avenue toward Riker's.

Phillip hit a bus stop sign, which waved back and forth, so Al jumped up on a wooden shelf for newspapers that was in front of a candy store and knocked it down. The Greek rushed out of the store and grabbed Al, and Al had to give him a dollar.

Later, when we were sitting in Riker's at the counter eating eggs, Ryko told me that Betty-Lou had taken a great dislike to Phillip.

"There's something rotten about him," she had said. "He has the smell of death about him."

"That's one for the book all right," I said.

Later, as we were leaving Riker's, Phillip showed me a dollar and said he'd stolen it out of Betty-Lou's purse.

8

MIKE RYKO

W<small>EDNESDAY TURNED OUT TO BE A BEAUTIFUL DAY</small>.
It was one of those clear and cool June days when everything is blue and rose and turret-brown. I stuck my head
out Janie's bedroom window and looked around. It was
eleven o'clock yet everything looked fresh and keen like
early morning.

Janie was sore at Phillip and me for coming home
late, so she didn't get up to make us breakfast, and Barbara was home in Manhasset.

We started off for the Union Hall and just as we
turned down 17th Street there was Ramsay Allen, waiting for us on the steps of the hall with a big smile on
his face.

We went in the hall and there was a whole flock of
new jobs on the board. The first thing I did was go back
in one of the offices and start beefing about my card.

"I can't get a ship with this member-in-arrears card," I told the official, "and I've got to go right away because I'm broke."

"Can't do anything for you," he said flatly.

I went back to Phillip and Al. They were sitting in a row of chairs and Phillip was reading Briffault's *Europa* while Al watched him. I told them what the official had said.

Al said he knew a girl from the Village who worked in one of the offices upstairs. "I'll try to cook something up," he said, and went upstairs to see her.

He got back fifteen minutes later and told us he had made an appointment with her for lunch.

Phillip said, "What are you going to pay her lunch with?"

Al said he'd be back in a half hour with some money, and he left.

"Well," I said to Phillip, "I wonder why he's helping us?"

"He probably thinks I'll let him ship out with me," said Phil.

It was about a quarter to one when Al got back with five bucks he had borrowed from some friends in the Village. He went upstairs and came down again with the union girl. It was plain to see that this girl was stuck on Al, and maybe she would do anything for him.

We started off for lunch and went into a Spanish restaurant on Eighth Avenue. The girl said she ate here every day and that it was a real "mañana" place. Then she asked me what my problem was and I told her.

"You see," I concluded, "the reason why I'm behind in dues and overstayed my leave is because I was down with the flu for two weeks and it sort of knocked me off my stride."

"Didn't you tell them that?"

"Well," I said, "I didn't think it would make any difference."

"Oh yes," she said, "even if it was only for two weeks."

Then I started ingratiating myself with her by asking if she knew such-and-such in the Village, or had she met such-and-such, giving her a list of my old-time left-wing friends. She knew some of them. Then I began to overdo it, telling her about my communist activities in Pennsylvania and how once I'd been arrested on the Boston Common as an agitator. She was impressed by all this. She figured me as one of the boys.

Then Al started telling funny stories, and the luncheon developed into a miniature party, only Phillip almost botched the whole works by laughing when she mentioned "the common man."

Finally Al made a date with her for next week, and that sort of clinched the whole deal. When we were finished she wiped her mouth with a paper napkin and said, "Well I think I can do something about that card of yours, Mike."

So we all went back to 17th Street and she told us to wait while she made a few interoffice calls. "I'll have definite news for you by three o'clock," she said, and we saw her to the Union Hall door.

In the Anchor Bar, we ordered a round of beers, and when Phillip went into the men's room Al said to me, "Well, Mike, so you're headed for France. I sure wish I could come along."

"Why don't you?" I said.

"Phillip wouldn't have it, I don't think. What do you think?"

"We haven't talked about it. As far as I'm concerned I'd like to have you along. The more the merrier, and with you around we'd make a better go of it on the tramp, I imagine."

"Yes," said Al nodding his head, "I think the three of us would make a better go of it. Both of you are young and impractical, you wouldn't know how to get food or money."

"That's logical," I said. "Alone I imagine we'd starve."

"I believe you're right," Al said. Then he went on: "Mike, why don't you persuade Phillip to let me come along?"

"Well," I said, "it's okay with me, as I told you. And I guess there's nothing to lose trying to persuade Phillip, he may relent. Sure, I'll ask him."

"Give him all the arguments about food and money."

"Yeah," I said.

"Do that, Mike."

"I will."

Al patted me on the shoulder and ordered me another beer.

Phillip got back, and he and Al began talking about the New Vision again. Phil was wondering maybe it was impossible to achieve since we were all equipped with a limited number of senses.

Al nodded his head and said, "That's interesting. But you might find a great deal of interesting occultist material in Yeats and also in cabalistic doctrine."

"Rimbaud thought he was God," Phillip said. "Maybe that's the primary requisite. In cabala man stands on the threshold of vegetable life, and between him and God remains only a misty shroud. But suppose you actually projected yourself as God, as the sun, then what would you see and know?"

"Yes," said Al. "You might have something there.

But of course Rimbaud eventually failed after a projection of that sort."

Phillip knotted his fist. "Of course he did, and I think I understand why, though I'm not certain I could explain it coherently."

"Well try anyway," Al persuaded gently and knitted his brow.

Here Phillip waved the matter away and asked for more beer.

Finally it was three o'clock, and we went back across the street into the hall. I called up the girl from the foyer and she told me who to see. I thanked her for her trouble and then Al took the phone and started chatting with her.

The union official said she had heard of my special case from a sister, and due to the circumstances she was willing to issue me a new card. While it was being made out, I slipped a couple of blank cards in my pocket in case of any future emergency.

I went back to Phillip and Al with the good news. We stood in front of the board with the other seamen and looked over the shipping.

"Now we'll get a ship for sure," Phillip said.

"If not today, tomorrow," I said. Then I showed Al the blank cards I had lifted from the office. He immediately took them out of my hand and stuffed them into his coat pocket. It was done so quickly that Phillip hadn't even noticed. I looked at Al and he looked at me gravely.

A minute later Al said he had to leave to go do a painting job on 52nd Street, and he left. Phillip and I sat down on a bench to wait for the three-thirty job call.

At three-thirty there was a call for deckhands. I threw in my new card with four other ABs and almost flopped when one of the jobs was sold to me. Phillip and I beamed with satisfaction, and he lit my cigarette with trembling hands.

Then the call for ordinary seamen came, and Phillip threw in his card with about ten other ordinaries. The dispatcher was shuffling the cards around, checking on seniority dates.

There was one of these ordinaries who had been hanging around the job window all day, a thin, pimply kid of about seventeen who looked like some sort of moron. His card was thrown back in his face, as had been the case all day long. I looked at his card and saw 'member in arrears' stamped on it. He didn't have enough sense to go to the open job window, so he just hung around this window all day long, throwing in his worthless card and getting it thrown back in his grimly smiling face. I told him what to do, since no one else seemed to bother about it, not even the dispatcher.

Phillip's card was thrown back, but he was beaten only by a matter of hours in seniority. We went back to our seats and I said, "It'll come."

The dispatcher was saying over the mike, "One of those AB jobs returned. One AB job open." That was mine.

"Tomorrow's our day," I said. "We'll get up real early." I started to think about Al's success with the union girl, and looked at Phillip, who had reopened his book.

"Al's an amazing guy," I said. "With him you never have to worry about anything."

Phillip looked up from his book.

I decided to get it over with so I said, "Why don't you let Al ship out with us? He wants to come bad."

Phillip made a tortured face. "Eee," he said, "no. The whole purpose of shipping out is to get away from him. I told you that."

I shrugged and said, "I don't get it."

"Since you're not very well acquainted with the facts I don't expect you to get it."

"Okay," I said coldly.

It got to be five o'clock again, and Phillip suggested we go to Al's and have dinner with him. He thought that Al would have some money from painting, but I knew damned well Al was running all over town looking for a time-clock puncher with which to stamp his blank cards so he could ship out with us.

When we got to Al's place, over a jazz club on 52nd Street, he wasn't home yet. I stretched out on the couch and Phil sat in the easy chair to read *Europa*.

From the couch I could see the backyard where there was an old vine-covered plaster wall with a crack in it that looked beautiful in the clear late-afternoon light. I said to Phil, "Look at that wall outside, and the exotic vine leaves. I'll bet that's what Montmartre looks like."

Phillip went to the French window and stood looking out at the wall. Pretty soon I fell asleep on the couch.

When I woke up, Al and Phillip were standing over the couch telling me to get up. I turned over and started to think about a dream I'd just had. It was about some hills I'd seen in Tennessee. Then I reflected how odd it was that I wasn't dreaming about ships at all these days, because whenever I go to sea I dream about it beforehand.

A while later the door opened just a few inches and Will Dennison slipped in his six-foot-three shadow. I was startled because he had come in without a sound. He was wearing a seersucker coat, and a cigarette hung half-smoked from his mouth. He sat down in the easy chair and Al and Phillip began telling him about our luncheon with the union girl and how it had all worked out. I sat up on the couch and watched Dennison's reaction.

There wasn't ever much reaction to note in Dennison. I had known him for several months and still couldn't make him out. He hailed from Reno, Nevada, and he had a look about him that suggested racetracks and gambling tables. But that was the external impression only. He spoke in a slow surly drawl that had an incongruous tint of refinement to it. And I knew that he was involved in all kinds of shady activities. He was always getting mysterious phone calls from Chicago, and some of the guys that visited him in his apartment seemed pleasant enough except that they had a tight, secret look about them.

It seemed that Will had an old lady who still lived in Reno and kept sending him packages of food, and that every Christmas, according to Phillip and Al, he always packed up and took a trip west. There was something distinctively western about Dennison, and I often wondered why he stayed in the East. Of course there was some talk about the unhealthy atmosphere out West for him, where it was rumored he had put something over on a number of people who would be glad to see him sometime. Evidently, his annual Christmas journey was on the q.t.

Dennison reminded me of a cowboy, somehow. But

not the cowboy you see in the movies on a white horse with a pearl-gray Stetson and a heavily ornamented double holster. Will is the cowboy who wears a plain vest and half-Stetson, who is always sitting at a card table in the saloon and withdrawing silently with his money when the hero and the villain start shooting it out.

9

WILL DENNISON

WEDNESDAY NIGHT WAS THE SAME STORY. WHEN I got to Al's on my way home from work, there sat Ryko and Phillip. It seems they had slept late so couldn't get a ship, but tomorrow for sure and so forth. I was getting disgusted and could see this thing running on for weeks. We started off for dinner.

In the hall I ran into Agnes. She had spent the day interviewing people down at the House of Detention and found out for sure that Hugh was really there. Next day she planned to get a lawyer for him so he could get out on bail. She had quit her job so as to give all her time to the matter. I gave her the name of a lawyer I knew who got a friend of mine off with two months after he had been caught inside an office building at four a.m. with $1,500 in his pocket that didn't belong to him.

I asked Agnes if she would join us for dinner but she said no, she was broke. I said, "On me," and she still said no. She was always like that. So I said good night and walked out.

The others were standing in the street in front of the house.

I said, "Agnes wouldn't come for dinner because she is broke. Some people have some pride."

Phillip said, "People get silly ideas."

"Yeah," I said, "but you're an artist. You don't believe in decency and honesty and gratitude. Where shall we eat?"

Phillip said he wanted to go to the Fifth Avenue Playhouse and see *Pépé le Moko* after dinner, so we decided to eat in the Village. We took the Seventh Avenue subway down to Sheridan Square and went in Chumley's to eat. Phillip started right off ordering Pernod and daiquiris.

After dinner we walked to the Fifth Avenue Playhouse. Phillip and Ryko got in for half price when they showed merchant marine papers. When we were in the theater Phillip went in the row first and sat down, Ryko went next, then me, then Al last.

During the movie Al kept craning his neck to look across at Phillip, and finally moved to the other side of the front row next, where he had an unobstructed view of Phillip's profile.

After the movie we went to MacDonald's Tavern, which is a queer place, and it was packed with fags all screaming and swishing around. Every now and then one of them would utter a shrill cry.

We pushed our way to the bar and ordered some drinks. The older fags were looking frankly at Phillip, but the younger ones pretended not to notice him and stood around in groups, talking and looking at him out of the corner of their eyes.

There were several sailors standing around and I heard one of them say, "Where are the women in this fucking town?"

A well-dressed middle-aged man started talking to Phillip about James Joyce and told Phillip he didn't know anything about literature, trying to establish himself in a position of dominance. Then he bought Phillip a drink.

A little thin black-haired man with a slightly in-sane grin on his face came up to Al and asked him for a cigarette. Al produced the package and there was only one cigarette in it. The man said, "The last cigarette. Well, I'll take it," which he did.

Al looked at him coldly and turned his head away.

The man began to explain that in the Village you had to act like a character. He was from Hartford, Connecticut, and looking for a woman. Then he caught sight of two lesbians who were standing by the piano, and his eyes glistened.

"Women!" he said.

He went over and stood behind them, looking at them with his insane grin.

We left MacDonald's and went around the corner to Minetta's.

Phillip said, "I wonder what Babs and Janie are doing tonight?" and Ryko said, "Well, we'll see them later."

The usual assortment of stupid characters was assembled in Minetta's. Joe Gould was sitting at a table. A man bumped into Al and said he was sorry.

Al said, "That's quite all right."

The man said, "I apologized because I'm a gentleman, but you wouldn't know about that."

Al looked at him, and the man said, "It so happens that I was intercollegiate boxing champion at the University of Michigan."

Nobody said anything and after a while the champion wandered away to bother somebody else. People in bars are always claiming to be boxers, hoping thereby to ward off attack, like a black snake will vibrate its tail in leaves and try to impersonate a rattlesnake.

Everyone had a few drinks. Al sat down with a fairly good-looking girl and began to talk to her. Phillip was standing at the bar, and I saw him showing his seaman's papers to someone who was trying to show him a document proving something about what he did in the last war.

I sat down with Al and the girl. It was hard work talking to her. Al was telling her about the movie, and I mentioned that I had been to Algiers.

At this the girl looked at me with great hostility and demanded, "When were you in Algiers?"

I said, "In 1934."

She continued to look at me with an expression of stupid suspicion and anger.

I began to get a feeling familiar to me from my bartending days of being the only sane man in a nuthouse. It doesn't make you feel superior but depressed and scared, because there is nobody you can contact. Right then I decided to go home.

I said, "Well Al, I have to get up early tomorrow. I think I'll go along." So I got up and left and started to walk home.

As I was walking past Tony Pastor's I saw Pat, the lesbian bouncer, throw a drunken young sailor out into the street. The sailor said, "That place is full of fucking queers." He swung at the air and nearly fell on his face, then he staggered away, muttering to himself.

I walked over to Seventh Avenue, then up to Christopher Street to buy the morning papers. On my way back I saw there was an argument in front of George's, so I crossed over to see what was going on.

The proprietor was standing in the doorway arguing with three people he had just thrown out of the joint. One of the men kept saying, "I write stories for the *Saturday Evening Post*."

The proprietor said, "I don't care what you do, Jack, I don't want you in my place. Now beat it," and he advanced on the group. They shrank away, but when the proprietor turned to go back in, the man who wrote for the *Saturday Evening Post* came forward again and the whole process was repeated.

As I walked away the proprietor was saying, "Why don't you go somewhere else? There are plenty of other places in New York."

I had the feeling that all over America such stupid arguments were taking place on street corners and in bars and restaurants. All over America, people were pulling credentials out of their pockets and sticking them under someone else's nose to prove they had been somewhere or done something. And I thought someday everyone in America will suddenly jump up and say "I don't take any shit!" and start pushing and cursing and clawing at the man next to him.

10

MIKE RYKO

AT TEN O'CLOCK THURSDAY MORNING PHILLIP threw a glassful of water in my face and said, "Come on, get up."

I was sleeping on the couch with all my clothes on, and Janie was sleeping in the bedroom. Phillip was all washed and combed and ready to go.

I was still half asleep when we got to the Union Hall, fortified by a cup of coffee and a sandwich from a Greek lunch cart.

There was a call for a whole deck crew just as we walked into the hall. We ran up to the window and I threw in my card with six other ABs. There were only seven cards for nine jobs so I was certain to get a job at last. But the dispatcher threw back two cards, one of which was mine.

"What the hell's wrong with my card?" I yelled through the cage.

"Yeah!" another AB wanted to know.

"There was a meeting last night," said the dispatcher, "and you didn't attend. Next time you'll know there was a meeting, brothers."

I grabbed another AB's card from the window and looked at the back of it. It was stamped "Attended Meeting June 26, 1944."

I went back to sit on a bench and swear.

Phillip was standing over me. "Well, what's next?" he asked.

I looked up at him a little helplessly, and then I said, "We'll have to figure something out."

We sat around and thought for a while, then I decided to pull something I knew would work. "Come on," I said to Phillip, and led him into one of the offices in back.

There was a union official sitting and talking over a phone. I leaned my hands on his desk and waited for his full attention. He kept on talking for ten minutes and then hung up.

I said, "Look, brother, I was just now getting a job when the dispatcher threw my card back and said it wasn't stamped for last night's meeting. Does that mean I can't get a ship?"

"It means you'll have to go to the open job window, brother."

"Well neither one of us"—I turned and gestured at Phillip—"could attend last night's meeting because we were in Washington. We'd been down there a couple of days to sit in on the Senate and House debates over the Pillsbury postwar bill. You see, we got drunk and decided to go down there—"

"What'd you think of the debates?" the official interrupted.

"Why," I said, turning to Phillip, "Phil and I've never seen anything like it. It was outrageous to sit and listen to those southern Democrat poll-tax reactionary bastards like John of Georgia and Banken of Mississippi make speeches against a bill like Pillsbury's."

The union official had a faint smile on his face. I was going to say something else when the phone rang. The official was busy for a minute, then he hung up and I started again. "So like I say—"

"Let's see the cards," he interrupted me and held out his hand. We gave him the cards and he stamped them.

"Thanks," I said gravely, like a brother just bailed out of jail by the union after a strike.

We walked out. I looked at the cards. They were stamped "Attended Meeting June 26, 1944."

"That was pretty good," Phil said.

"The psychology," I said, "is that they want as many intelligent liberals on the ships as possible, to spread around the dogma and to convert simple dopes into mouthpieces for the working class. What he's practically saying to us is 'spread it around, boys.'"

We found Ramsay Allen looking for us in the hall and told him about the union official. Al nodded appreciatively. Then, while Phillip was in the foyer buying cigarettes, I asked Al what he was going to do about the blank cards.

"I won't do anything," he said. "Phillip said he wouldn't let me on the same ship with him. It's no use."

I shrugged my shoulders and felt better.

Phillip came back and we stood around looking at the shipping board.

"I feel it in my bones," I said to Phillip. "We get our ship today or tomorrow."

Al was looking at Phillip all the time, and Phillip wouldn't pay any attention to him. Finally he said to Al, "Why don't you spend the afternoon getting money instead of hanging around here."

Al said, "Well yes, that's an idea. I could do a little calcimining for old Mrs. Burdett."

"Well go ahead, then," Phillip said, and Al immediately left.

Phil and I had a little lunch and some beer at the Anchor Bar, waited around for jobs in the hall, read, dozed on the benches, and finally it was almost closing time again. We had passed up several jobs on tankers because we wanted to go on a freighter. Now that our cards were good, we were getting fussy. Tankers that went to France stayed offshore and we wouldn't be able to jump ship.

Allen got back just before five o'clock and showed us a ten-dollar bill.

"Well, well," Phillip said, "don't tell me you made all that."

Al showed us two pawn receipts for two small brilliants. Phillip wanted to know where Al had gotten the brilliants.

Al said, "I did a paint job for old Mrs. Burdett while she was out with her dog, and I found these in a dresser drawer. Her two cats were watching me."

"You mean that old Mrs. Burdett from Memphis you always have tea with when you run out of money?"

"Yes," said Al, "an old friend of the family's."

"Well, nice going," Phillip said. "Now let's spend it."

"No ship?" Al inquired brightly.

Phillip said, "Tomorrow's another day."

We stopped first at the Anchor Bar and each had a whiskey and soda. The place was jammed with seamen who had gotten jobs during the day and who were drinking and loading on for the long voyage.

We decided to go and see a French picture on Times Square and took the subway. When we got there we looked around until we found an Italian spaghetti joint and went into it.

Al and I ordered two bottles of beer and Phil ordered a sherry. He had bought a *P.M.* and was looking at the military map as he drank his sherry and talking about the front. Then our spaghetti arrived. I went over to the counter and got a big shaker of paprika to put on my meat sauce.

After we'd finished eating, Phil pushed the shaker of paprika to Al across the table and said loudly, "Come on, Allen, let's see you eat a spoonful of this stuff. Keats did it."

Al said, "Well, I don't know,"

"It cleans out your stomach," Phil was saying, so that the people at the next table heard him. "It'll be good for your ulcers. If Keats did it, why don't you?"

So Al took a large spoon that you eat spaghetti with and shook some red paprika into it. Then he took in the whole mouthful and held it in his mouth. His eyes began to water and he was trying to smile.

"Here," said Phillip, pushing a glass of water across the table, "take water with it. Makes it worse."

I handed Al some bread and said, "Take bread and get the pepper down."

"Water makes it worse," Phillip insisted. "Bread is a compromise."

So Al drank the water, and the tears were running down his cheeks, he was burning so much. Every now and then he'd shake his head and say "Whoo!" and then smile at Phillip. It was very annoying and I insisted that Al take bread.

"This isn't getting us anywhere," I said, but they didn't listen.

So Al went on saying "Whoo!" and smiling at Phillip, just like an idiot who is burning at the stake and smiles and shakes his head and says "Boy! This hurts!" to his tormentors.

Finally the incident sort of spoofed out, and we got up and Al paid the check.

As we were walking out of the joint, Phillip picked up a long reed of macaroni from the cook's display in the window and carried it out like a cane. When we were on the sidewalk, he put the end of the reed against his fly and it looked just like a shimmering spurt of piss. Men going by in the evening rush stared until they saw it was only macaroni, and they moved on without a pause. Women turned their heads away and pretended not to notice. Phillip walked toward the Apollo theater holding it against his fly and looked like a guy who was taking a piss as he walked.

Al bought the tickets and we walked into the Apollo theater. We went upstairs to the balcony so that we could smoke as we watched the movie.

Just at the alcove to the right of the balcony, there is usually a group of fags hanging around, looking half of the time at the picture and the rest of the time along the balcony seats for any good prospects. They were standing there giving us the side glance as we came up the stairs, when Phillip ran up to the sand jar and began holding the macaroni to his fly and shaking it in the sand, so that it looked like he was pissing diffusely into the sand jar. The fags glided away like crayfish.

We went down and got seats in the first row of the balcony and lit up cigarettes.

Port of Shadows is about a French army deserter who is in Le Havre, trying to skip the country. Everything is set, he has a passport and is on a ship, when he gets the idea to go back and see his girl once again before he sails. The result is a gangster shoots him in the back and the ship sails without him. The last scene shows the ship sailing out of Le Havre without him.

During the showing of the picture Al, who was sitting between Phillip and me, was very quiet. When it was over I turned to him and asked him how he'd liked it.

"It's the best picture I ever saw," he said, and I noticed his eyes were moist.

We sat through another picture, a British film, and in the middle of it Al went out and came back five minutes later with three cartons of cold chocolate milk. Phillip grabbed his carton and drank it up without speaking. I thanked Al for mine.

After the show, we came out of the theater and walked toward Eighth Avenue to have a few drinks.

At the corner of Eighth Avenue and 42nd Street, a thin old man with white hair had stationed himself in the middle of the sidewalk and was looking up at the sky with clasped hands. Every now and then, someone would stop and look up. When they saw nothing was there, they walked on without any comment or change of expression. Mostly they just walked by and didn't see him. I guess he was praying.

We went into a bar on Eighth Avenue near 43rd Street. There were some greasy, shady-looking characters in dark suits, a gambler with a loud tie and a diamond ring, several whores, a sprinkle of fags, and crowds of servicemen. Against this backdrop the young servicemen looked jarringly out of place, as though they had invaded a foreign country or some ruins.

We stayed there for a while, drinking beer because we didn't feel like getting drunk, then we left and took the subway down to Washington Square. Al was a little uneasy at this point because he knew he would not be welcome at Apartment 32.

When we got there we found Janie and Barbara. They had just had a cup of coffee at the Waldorf Cafeteria after waiting for Phillip and me for hours, and now they were in an unfriendly mood.

"Where the hell have you been?" Janie wanted to know.

I sat down in a chair with the cat in my lap, Phil sat on the couch beside Barbara, and Al sat on the white hassock in the middle of the room and smiled all round. When Janie went into the kitchen to get food for the cat, Al jumped up and said, "May I help you?"

I turned on the radio to some loud dance music because everybody was being so unpleasant and tense. Barbara was sulking, and Phil was thumbing through a copy of Faulkner's *Sanctuary*. I lay down on the other couch and started to take a nap.

I woke up just in time to hear Janie yell "Go home!" and throw a book at Al. It hit him on the shoulder. Barbara was already gone home and Phillip was stretched out on the couch. The bedroom door slammed after Janie.

Al looked down questioningly at Phillip.

"You might as well," Phillip said.

Al said, "Well, good night," and walked out of the apartment.

I went into the bedroom and closed the door after me.

"Him out there," Janie said when I started undressing, "you'd better watch out for him."

"Who?"

"Mr. Phillip."

"What's the matter with him?"

"You know why he wants to ship out with you, don't you?"

I threw my pants on the chair and said, "No, why?"

"Because he's a queer and wants to make you."

"What?" I said.

"Don't 'what' me. Some night at sea when he jumps on you, you'll know what I was talking about."

I sighed, shook my head, and gave her a pitying look.

She said, "Ramsay Allen knows him better than you do, so go ahead and be a know-it-all."

"You're nuts," I said.

"You've been living with me for a whole year, you've been promising to marry me, I've been giving you money, now you start hanging around with a bunch of queers and don't come home at night."

"So that's who's been buzzing in your ear," I said, "Ramsay Allen. Don't you know he'd say or do anything to break up this trip?"

Janie started to yell. "First thing I'll know you'll be a goddamned queer yourself. Maybe you are already."

I said, "What makes you believe anything that Al tells you?"

"You've been laying this Helen bitch, you've been giving her money but you never give me anything."

I said, "Who gave you *that* idea?"

"You think I'm stupid," she said. "You think I don't know what's going on around here."

"Well, what?"

"You're going to go to Reno with that gambler Dennison, that's what. You think you're going to get rid of me, but you won't get away with it."

I said, "Oh, for Christ's sake."

Then I turned quickly sideways as she brought her knee up to my balls. She followed up by punching me on the side of the face with her hard, thin knuckles. So I k-norcked her one with the palm of my hand.

There was a small table by the side of the bed that had a big ashtray heaped with cigarette butts and ashes on it, and books, papers, an alarm clock, empty glasses, bottles of perfume, nail files, a deck of cards, and a container of talcum powder. Janie hit the edge of the table on her way down and tipped it over so that the contents spilled all over her. She was lying there spitting out cigarette butts, with ashes and talcum powder all over her face and her dress up over her knees.

"You bastard!" she screamed. "You're trying to mar my beauty!"

So I went out into the other room.

Phillip was sitting up on the couch. "Darling," he said in a loud voice, "I can't hide my love any longer."

I said, "Shut up, for Christ's sake."

From the bedroom we could hear sobs.

After a while I went back to Janie. She was still sitting on the floor so I slung her up on the bed and started kissing her.

A few minutes later she got up and fixed her face. She came back on the bed with me and said, "When you get back from this trip, we'll get a new apartment."

The next morning Phillip and I managed to get up fairly early, and Janie, now at peace with both of us, fried a bacon-and-egg breakfast and then sent us off. She was going to spend the day cleaning up the apartment.

Just before closing time at the Union Hall, Phil and I got our ship. It was the S.S. *Harvey West*, a Liberty ship, and it was laying over in Hoboken.

"Report tomorrow morning at eight o'clock," said the dispatcher, "and bring all your gear."

We went back into the office and picked up our job slips.

"Well," said Phillip, "this is it."

"Yeah," I said, "let's celebrate."

11

WILL DENNISON

FRIDAY NIGHT AFTER WORK I MET HELEN AND WE went back to my apartment. But Al, Phillip, and Ryko were waiting on my doorstep. I said hello to Al and looked at Mike and Phillip in disgust, without saying anything.

Phillip said, "Well, we're shipping out tomorrow. We've been assigned to a ship and report at the pier tomorrow morning."

I said, "Can I count on that? I'm getting sick of these abortive departures."

"This is for sure. Now in view of the fact that we are leaving, why don't you make a generous gesture and take us all to dinner?"

"If I could be sure you were really going I'd take you to the Colony—since I can't be sure, we will compromise and eat here." I started upstairs with Helen and they all followed.

Helen sat down in the easy chair before Phillip could. I went over to the desk and got a piece of paper. "I'll make out a list," I said.

"How about some steak?" said Al. "I saw some on Bleecker Street."

"Okay," I said. "And get a quart of Dubonnet and seltzer water." I wrote the items down. "Some bleu cheese, Italian bread, butter, apples, and don't forget to get some ice for the Dubonnet." I handed Al the list.

"How about some rum?" said Phillip.

"No," I said. "Dubonnet is a better summer drink. Besides, I don't want to spend the money."

Phillip said, "Don't be bourgeois, Dennison. After all, we're shipping out tomorrow. You may never see us again."

"I'm the later bourgeois Rimbaud," I said. "And if you don't come back, I'll always remember you just the way you look now."

I gave Al ten dollars. Phillip started to rummage through my bureau drawer and said he wanted to put on some shorts.

"Yes," said Al, leaping up, his joints creaking audibly, "a wonderful idea!"

I kept a sharp eye on Phillip until he had fished out two pairs of the shorts I used occasionally to work out in a gymnasium. He handed Al a pair of the shorts, and they changed right there in the middle of the room.

Helen said, "Don't mind me, fellows."

I said, "Do you guys intend to go out on the public streets dressed like that?"

Al said, "Of course."

I turned to Ryko. "You better take the ten dollars and do the shopping. These two imbeciles will get picked up for indecent exposure."

Ryko took the ten dollars and the shopping list and they all left. "Don't forget the ice," I said as they walked out the door.

I gave my full attention to Helen, but she kept saying the others would be back any time and I said that didn't make any difference to me. And she said, "After all," coyly, and I got disgusted.

Phillip came back after a few minutes with a small package containing the wine.

I said, "Where's the ice? Where's the seltzer? That stuff isn't fit to drink without seltzer and ice."

Phillip said, "Oh I sent Al to get the ice. It comes in big heavy chunks, you know. Ryko is getting the rest of the stuff." He was rummaging through the desk drawer. "Where the hell's the corkscrew?"

I told him there wasn't one, he'd have to borrow it from the landlady, so he went upstairs.

Someone kicked at the door. I opened it and there was Ryko with packages in both arms. He said, "Jesus, I was embarrassed walking around with those two guys in their shorts. I thought the Bleecker Street wops would start something. They were whistling at them."

I began opening the packages and pulling the stuff out. There were several beautiful thick steaks, some bleu cheese, fresh and moist, a small bag of apples, a long piece of Italian bread. I held out the apples and said, "These go very well with cheese."

Ryko was sitting down on the couch, and he said, "Yeah."

Phillip came back with a corkscrew. I said, "Let me do that," and took the bottle between my knees and opened it, which made a loud pop.

Phillip said, "Hasn't Al gotten back with the ice yet? What's the matter with him?"

Helen was sitting there smoking, with her legs crossed so that you could see her thighs. I sat down and rubbed her leg. Phillip asked her for a cigarette and she gave him one, holding the package at arm's length. He took it and said, "Thanks." She didn't answer and turned her head.

At this point, Al came in, pushing through the half-open door with his shoulder, rushed over to the basin, and dropped a large piece of ice wrapped in newspapers into it. He stood there rubbing his numb hands together. Then he playfully tried to place his cold hands on Phillip, who twisted away.

I said, "Where's the seltzer?"

Ryko got up and said he would go out and get the seltzer. So I went over to the basin, chopped up the ice with a throwing knife I used for all purposes, and put ice into five glasses. Then I poured a slug of Dubonnet into each glass. By the time I had finished with this, Ryko was back with the seltzer. I squirted seltzer into each glass.

"Everybody help themselves," I said and grabbed myself the glass that had the most Dubonnet in it. I also grabbed a glass and handed it to Helen. I was thirsty from working all day, and I refilled my glass before anyone else had hardly started.

I paused in the middle of my second glass and said, "Who's going to cook this steak?"

Al said he would cook it. There was a gas stove in the hall on the top floor.

Phillip said, "Mother Allen is so reliable." Then he picked up a steak without any paper on it and started out the door beckoning with his hand that had the steak draped over it.

Al picked up the other steaks and some butter and bounded out after him.

I finished my drink and poured another one. Ryko was reading T. S. Eliot on the couch, and I began to neck with Helen and feel up her leg. She didn't have any slip on, but she stopped my hand before I could get it all the way up.

After a few minutes Phillip came down and sat on the floor with his *Europa*.

I said, "You ought to read the whipping scene in that book. It's the only good thing in it."

Ryko said, "Is Al all alone up there?"

Phillip said, "How should I know? I'm not there, am I?"

Ryko got up.

"Where you going?" I asked.

He said, "I think I'll go upstairs and help," and he went out.

A minute later Phillip snapped his book to and went back upstairs.

I poured a weak Dubonnet for Helen and a strong one for myself. I was making sure I got enough.

Finally, Ryko came down with the first piece of steak on a plate. He placed it on the arm of my chair and said, "Isn't it a bitch?" and I said, "Yeah."

I didn't see a knife around, and my throwing knife isn't sharp enough to cut anything with, so I tore off a piece of steak for Helen and one for myself. Ryko tore off a piece too, and we all started to eat. Mine wasn't salty enough, so I went over and got some salt from on top of the icebox.

While I was getting some salt, I unwrapped the bread and wrenched a piece off, then I offered the loaf to Helen and Ryko with one hand while I crammed in a mouthful with the other hand. I was feeling a little tight, and very hungry.

At this point, Al and Phillip arrived, Al carrying a big frying pan with two steaks sizzling in it. He set the pan down on the electric plate to cool. Then he made Phillip a drink and handed it to him.

When the pan had cooled, Al placed it on the floor and he and Phillip sat down cross-legged facing each other with the steaks between them. Then Phillip started to growl like a leopard, picked up a big piece of steak, and tore at it with his teeth. Al reached for Phillip's steak, and Phillip made a clawing motion with his hand, growling and snarling. The steak blood ran down their chins and dripped on their legs.

I said to Ryko, "Did you see those pictures in *Life* of the lion that killed his brother over a piece of steak? It shows first the steak thrown into the cage, then one lion grabs it in his teeth and starts dragging it away toward a corner, then the other lion rushes over and tries to grab the steak, and the first lion clouts him one alongside the head—broke his neck. Last scene you see the lion rolled over on his back with his legs up in the air," and I stuck my hands up in the air and waved them to show how dead the lion was.

Ryko said, "Yeah? Must have been good."

I now decided I'd better get into the lion game if I was to get my steak, so I began to growl and snarl and ripped off a piece of steak. Everybody but Helen was growling, and I think Phillip growled the best.

The steak was gone, so I brought out the cheese. I'd had enough of the lion stuff by now. We ate the cheese and Italian bread and the apples, which is a marvelous combination. Then we sat back and lit cigarettes and finished up most of the Dubonnet.

Helen was sitting on my lap and I began to get a hard-on. Ryko kept looking at her legs from across the room.

"You're a sweet kid," I said in her ear.

We sat around a while longer, and then finally Helen got up and said she had to go back to Queens, pulling her dress down and twisting it around and smoothing it out.

"Leave the door open," Al said. "We need some air in here."

In the hall I asked Helen if she would meet me in Chumley's on Monday night, and she said, "Yes, if you're alone," and went down the stairs.

I went back into the room and started walking around. I had on my old seersucker coat that had a hole in the elbow, no bigger than a dime. Phillip suddenly stuck a forefinger in the hole and ripped down. The whole sleeve came off from the elbow down. So then Al leaped in like a jackal and began ripping the coat off my back. The coat was so old it tore like paper. Soon it was hanging on me in shreds.

So then I took off what was left of the coat and sat down and began tying the pieces together in a long rope. Phillip helped me and then Al began to do it, too. We made one long rope out of the whole coat and strung it around the room like a festoon. The four of us sat there looking at it.

After a while Phillip wanted to go out and drink in a bar. I decided not to go along, because I knew that the expense would fall on me. Ryko said he wanted to go to a whorehouse and Phillip said, "Yes, Dennison, why don't you treat us to a whorehouse?"

I said, "What's the matter with you young fellows, can't you get women for yourselves?—all those Washington Square college girls over there walking around with the juice dripping down their legs. Why, when I was your age, I was like a young bull. If I had a mind to it, I could tell you stories that'd make your cock stand." I limped over like an old man and dug Phillip in the ribs and cackled.

Then I straightened up and dropped the old-man act and said to him, "Why don't you lay Barbara?"

"I don't know. She's a virgin."

Al said, "Well, Phillip, I don't think you want to lay her."

Phillip looked at Al. "It's not that. She doesn't know what she wants. She's all mixed up."

Ryko said from across the room, "You've been necking with her for months. Why don't you just up and fuck her?"

Al ignored this remark and looked at Phillip seriously. "I don't see why you always have to get in these complicated emotional entanglements with women. Why can't you develop a simple attitude toward them?"

Yeah, I said to myself, *why can't we do away with women altogether.*

Aloud I said, "Al's right, my boy." I assumed a Lionel

Barrymore tone of voice. "Women, Phillip, are the root of all evil."

We heard some tittering out in the hall, and a dollar bill all crumpled up sailed into the room and bounced on the floor at Ryko's feet.

"Whorehouse money," a girl's voice said.

Ryko said, "It's Janie." He jumped up on his feet. "And Barbara too." He started toward the door and we heard feet running down the stairs. "Where are you going?" Ryko yelled. "Hey!"

Phillip and Al were on their feet. Al was looking at Phillip indecisively. Ryko was out in the hall and a moment later we heard him yell, "Hey Phil, come on before they skip. They're running out on the street."

Phillip went out the door and Al hurried after him. I got up and strolled out to the head of the stairs.

Phillip was hollering to Ryko, who was now down at the street door, "Do you see them?"

Ryko yelled back, "No, I can't see them. They've gone toward Seventh Avenue."

Al said, "Well, if they're gone, I guess we'd better forget about it."

Phillip turned irritably. "Go to hell, you old fairy," he said and started running down the stairs.

Al hesitated a moment without looking at me, then ran down after them in long jumps over the steps.

I went back into the room and went to the window. Ryko was standing on the corner below, yelling at Phillip to hurry up. Then they disappeared around the corner, and I saw Al following swiftly, in his long, bounding walk.

I finished the last half inch of Dubonnet, closed the door, and sat down in the chair to smoke. I was thinking it was about time to brush my teeth when the buzzer rang. It was Phillip and Al.

Phillip said, "How about loaning me five dollars?"

"What for?" I asked.

"I gotta get a taxi and follow those wenches."

"Well," I said, "I'm sorry Phillip, but you catch me at a bad time." The whole thing seemed silly to me and I didn't like his tone, which was rather peremptory.

He said, "You've got it. Come on, let me have it."

I said, "I'm sorry," cold and dry.

He saw I meant it and got up. "Well, if you won't lend it to me, I guess I'll have to get it from somewhere else."

I said, "Very likely."

Al had been sitting there all the time without saying anything. Phillip walked out, and Al said good night to me at the door.

12

MIKE RYKO

PHILLIP AND AL CAME BACK FROM DENNISON'S AND
Phillip said he couldn't borrow any money from him.
I was sitting on Betty-Lou's bed, talking to her and ad-
miring her Oriental-looking nightgown. I had been
telling her how unhappy with Janie I was, and every
now and then I'd take her hand.

"Well," I said, "let's go back to George's. They may
be there."

"Who are you trying to find?" Betty-Lou asked.

"Some friends," I said and got up off the bed.

Al started talking to Betty-Lou, and she was just
about ready to climb out of bed and play the hostess
when Phillip walked out the door and Al and I followed.

We found Barbara wandering up Seventh Avenue.

"Where's Janie?" Phillip said. "What are you doing?"

Barbara was a little drunk and she said "George's,"

so we all went to George's and there was Janie, with a sailor buying her scotch and sodas. Both Barbara and Janie were dressed in their best, and both of them were a little drunk.

"You bastard," was the first thing Janie said to me, and then we had a few drinks and decided to run down to Minetta's.

The sailor was still standing around. He was looking at me. "What's the story?" he said.

"She's my wife," I said, and we all left.

On the way to Minetta's Al had to walk a few feet behind everyone because Janie and Barbara wouldn't let him walk with us. So he just followed in his long, loping stride, like a shadow.

We got to Minetta's and sat down at two different tables. Janie wouldn't let Al sit with her, and Barbara was sitting at Joe Gould's table with five or six other Minetta characters, so Al sat down at a table by himself.

Phillip was sitting next to Barbara and occasionally leaning his head on her shoulder. Then he suddenly got bored with the conversation there and walked to the bar alone, leaving Barbara with Joe Gould and the others. Al was right at Phillip's side and ordered two drinks.

Janie and I were sitting in a sort of sullen silence. I was sore at her because she wouldn't let Al sit with us. "The goddamned queer," she kept saying, and I kept saying, "So what, he's a good guy," and she kept answering to that, "Shut up, queer."

Then Phillip came over from the bar with a glass in his hand and sat down with Janie and me. Al hovered nearby and I smiled encouragingly to him. He edged over slowly and began pulling up a chair next to Phillip.

"Go away, you," Janie said, and Al backed off and went over to the bar. But in a minute he was back, hovering around our table like an anxious waiter.

Nobody said much of anything, except Barbara, who seemed to be having a good time listening to Joe Gould and basking in the suggestive dialogue around her.

Then Phillip wanted to go elsewhere, and Janie wanted to go home, although I wanted to stay and drink up the whole place. Janie had a lot of money with her, she had just cashed a trust-fund check. We finally started to get up, but then Phillip sat down again, so I ran over to the bar and ordered some drinks.

At this point, a bunch of Minetta characters had run out on Minetta Lane and started to conduct a ballet in front of the place. Phillip went out and sat down to watch, cross-legged in the middle of the little street. Al sat down beside him in the same fashion to watch also, turning occasionally and commenting to Phillip.

Meanwhile, Janie and I did some more drinking, and then a guy came up and started to talk to Janie about his art. He found a receptive listener, because Janie herself did a little painting, and pretty soon he was inviting her up to his studio to see his cubist work. She agreed to this. Then the artist got pretty bewildered because Janie told Phillip, Barbara, and myself to come along and see this guy's studio.

So we all trooped out with Al shadowing us and went down the street. A bunch of other people had somehow joined forces with us, and by the time we got into the artist's studio there were at least ten of us, including Joe Gould and his cane.

First somebody turned on the radio, and some dancing started. Janie and I went into a bedroom and started to neck on a bed, and then she said we might as well copulate. But I didn't want to, because everybody was walking through the room on their way to and from another room. Then a lot of beer showed up in carton containers, and Janie and I went out into the studio room proper and took two quart containers apiece.

We went back to the bedroom and started to drink the beer. I began acting silly and climbing out the window, and the first thing I knew there was Al climbing in from outside, through the window. He had been out to find Phillip and couldn't get back in, because the door was locked downstairs.

"Where is Phillip?" I asked.

"That's what I'd like to know," he said.

I stuck my head out the window to see how Al had managed it: the studio was just over the Swing Rendezvous nightclub, and Al had hauled himself up over the marquee.

Meanwhile, Barbara was in the other room necking with the artist while Joe Gould sat on a bed with a dark-haired girl in slacks. He was talking to her with his chin resting on the handle of his cane. Finally Barbara came out of the room looking all disheveled and went to a mirror. "He just asked for it," she said to Janie, "and he got it."

The artist was glaring at Barbara, then he came over to me and said, "There stands a young lady who came very close to being laid."

I registered appropriate awe, and then went out to the studio room to look at this guy's work. Al was opening doors all over the place, looking for Phillip. He even opened closet doors and poked his head inside.

All along the wall of the studio were hung paintings that the artist had done. They were done in vivid colors set in rigid forms, like cubes and squares and circles.

"How do you like them?" I asked Janie, and she said the colors were nice.

Then Phillip somehow reappeared and we all

decided to go back to Minetta's. The artist, meanwhile, was getting very nasty with everybody, and finally he went and opened the door for everybody to get out.

We all started to file out, and as we passed, the artist made insult after insult. He referred to Barbara's close shave, called Al a queer, and finally turned around to pick up a cat that was passing in the hallway. He took it by the tail and flung it down the stairs, but the cat landed on its feet and scampered away. I went up to the artist and said, "I'm going to k-norck you one for that," but he didn't hear my remark, so I let it go at that.

We went back to Minetta's, which was so crowded you couldn't elbow your way around, and stood in the middle of the crowd hollering for drinks. I finally appropriated four beers from the bartender. Cathcart and a few other NYU students had by this time showed up, and I began to get sick and tired of all the noise and pushing, so I decided to go home.

On my way to Apartment 32, I reeled to one side and fell on top of some ash barrels that were empty. I rolled on top of one of them and got deposited into the gutter. Then I got up and walked on home, feeling dizzy and limping from the bump on my shin.

When I got to Apartment 32 Phil and Barbara were on the bed in Janie's bedroom, so I undressed and fell down on the couch. I lay there for a while, riding an imaginary bicycle in an attempt to catch up with the room. A minute later the doorbell rang, and I heard Phil yell from the bedroom, "What a hell of a time!"

First thing I knew he was up and running around Apartment 32 naked and cursing and pacing the carpet, while the doorbell kept ringing. So I had to get up and open the door.

It was Janie and Cathcart, and both of them were pie-eyed. They stumbled in and actually fell at my feet, while Phil, mad as hell, rushed into my den and slammed the door after him.

I grabbed Janie and threw her on the couch. Then out from the bedroom came Barbara draped in a bedsheet and went over to Cathcart, who was sitting drunkenly on the other couch, and dropped on his lap with a simple grin on her face. She started kissing him violently and he looked a little bewildered.

Meanwhile Janie kept hitting me over the head with her shoe, and just as Phil came rushing out again from the den to run back into the bedroom and slam the door after him, I leapt up and put out the light so Janie wouldn't aim so well.

After that there were all kinds of door slammings and noises and mutterings and floor creakings, as if Apartment 32 were the very Whore House of Hell itself.

13

MIKE RYKO

PHILLIP AND I WOKE UP AT NOON THE NEXT DAY. We were already four hours late reporting to our ship, so we each took a cold shower, drank a whole can of tomato juice from the icebox, picked up our sea bags, and ran out of the apartment, leaving Barbara and Janie asleep. It was a very hot noon outside.

We took the subway up to 42nd Street and hurried around the corner to a bus terminal, where we just made the Hoboken bus.

When we got to Hoboken, the city was all covered over with a pall of hot gray smoke from a fire on the waterfront. Every now and then a piece of soot dropped down, like black snow in an ash-colored oven-hot sky.

We had to take another bus to get to our pier. When we got there the smoke was even thicker and our eyes were smarting. We crossed the street to the guardhouse at the gate of the pier and dropped our bags with a bang. A uniformed guard sauntered up.

"The *Harvey West*," I said, showing my job slip and Coast Guard pass.

"*Harvey West*?" the guard said. "Wait a minute." He went inside the guardhouse and made a phone call. Then he came back and said, "The *Harvey West* shifted docks this morning at seven. She's now at the foot of Montague Street, Pier 4, Brooklyn."

I turned to Phil and showed him the palm of my hand.

"Well," he said, "if she's in Brooklyn, let's go to Brooklyn."

So we picked up our bags and shuffled away.

"Goddamn it," I was saying. "They tell us it's in Hoboken and she shifts to Brooklyn. When we get to Brooklyn, she'll be in Manhattan. Nothing but chaos everywhere. Let's have a glass of beer."

"We haven't got enough money," Phil said, "and there's no time to lose."

We asked directions for getting back to New York the fastest way and were told to take the ferry.

We dropped our bags at our feet and leaned on the rail of the ferry. It moved away from the slip and headed for Manhattan, shimmering across the river. Over to our left we saw what was causing all the smoke

in Hoboken: a big warehouse and a merchant ship flying the Norwegian flag were on fire. Heavy clouds of
pale gray smoke were spewing out of the warehouse,
and black smoke was coming out of the freighter. The
firemen were all over the place with their little toy
hoses and squirts of water. I was wondering how the
fire had started.

Gradually we approached Manhattan. There was
a cool breeze that smelled of the sea, blowing from the
southern end of the river. The ferry eased into the slip,
rubbed sides with the timbers until they groaned, and
churned water to nose up to the gangway.

We picked up our bags and walked east toward midtown, stopping at a garage on Tenth Avenue for a drink
of water. There was nobody around the garage and we
couldn't find a men's room, so I undid a hose used to
wash cars with from a large faucet and we let the water
spill into our mouths and over our faces. There was still
nobody around and I said to Phil, "Some garage. We
ought to take a couple of wrenches."

Then we walked to Eighth Avenue and spent our
last dime on the subway down to Brooklyn. We got off
at Borough Hall, only on the wrong side, so that we had
to walk through a lot of clanging traffic with our sea
bags on our shoulders while the sun pressed down like

a hot flatiron. We finally found Montague Street and started toward the waterfront.

At the foot of Montague Street there is a stone arch that overspans the street at the point where it dips down to the piers. We passed under this like a couple of Foreign Legionnaires just in sight of the fort after a long march.

In front of Pier 4, I said to the guard, "Is the *Harvey West* here?"

"She sure is, son."

We showed him our identification papers.

"She's all yours, son."

We stomped across the floor of the cool, damp warehouse that smelled of coffee beans. There were hundreds of longshoremen loading on ships on both sides of the wharf. Winches screeched, foremen yelled, and a little truck trailing a string of wagons darted in front of Phil and me from around a corner and almost ran into us.

"Is that her?" Phil said, pointing to the right.

There was the great hull of a Liberty ship show-ing, at intervals where the shed doors were open, all streaked with oil and rust and with water pissing out of her scuppers.

"That's her," I said.

"Is she big!" he exclaimed, feasting his eyes on the ship as we walked nearer to the gangplank.

Then I heard some yelling behind us and turned and saw some seamen coming toward us, waving their hands. Some of them were carrying their sea bags. I recognized a few of them from the Union Hall.

"You guys goin' on this *Harvey West?*" one of them asked, dropping his bag.

"Yeah," I said.

He said, "I'm supposed to be goin' on as bosun. What about you?"

"AB and ordinary," I told him.

"Well listen," the bosun said, looking over my shoulder at Phil, "we're almost the whole deck crew right here." He turned and gestured to the five other guys with him. "Now, none of us here are goin' to sign on until we get the lay of the land."

"What's the matter?" I asked.

"I shipped out with the mate on this one before, and he is a bastard, let me tell you. The work's never good enough for him. Now, look. This ship's goin' upriver to Albany to load on, and then it's comin' back to New York and out. None of us has to sign on till it gets back, but they've already set out the articles up there. None of us guys intend to sign on till we get back from Albany, because the mate is a prick and we gotta see he acts right with us."

"Well," I said, "what will the mate say?"

"We're playin' it safe, all of us. All you do, you two guys, is lay low and say nothin'. The mate is a prick and none of us are gonna take any shit from him."

"I guess that's all right with us," I said.

"Okay," said the bosun, "that's what we wanted to talk to you about. So just lay low for a while and don't say anything."

"Okay," I said, "and after you." I moved aside from the gangplank and let the bosun go up first. The five guys followed and Phil and I took up the rear.

When we were aboard, I stepped quickly into an alleyway and led Phil to an empty fo'c'sle. "We might as well appropriate two lower bunks," I said. "Throw your gear in that locker."

I could see this was going to be some trip, all right. Trouble already.

"Now," I said to Phil, "I'll show you around."

I took him up to the bow and had him lean over and look at the anchor and then at the anchor chain. I showed him the jumbo block. "This thing weighs over a hundred pounds," I said, "and it's just one of the little gadgets you work with on deck."

Phil slapped the jumbo block and it didn't budge.

Then I took him topside to the bridge and showed him the wheelhouse, then belowdecks to the refrigerator storage. There was no padlock on the door, so we went in. There were whole cold roasts of beef and gallons of milk in cans.

Phil ripped off a piece of beef with his fingers. I ran topside for some glasses and came back a minute later and poured out some cold foaming milk from the cans.

"This is the balls," Phil said.

We were very thirsty and hungry from running all over in the hot sun, looking for the *Harvey West*.

After we had had our fill, I led Phil back up to our fo'c'sle and we undressed to take a shower. After that, we dried up with some clean towels I got from the Negro steward belowdecks in the linen locker. Then we fished some clean work clothes out of our sea bags and put them on.

"When do we work?" Phil wanted to know, and I told him probably not before tomorrow morning.

I stretched out on the bunk and turned on the bulkhead light over my pillow. I picked up a book and started to read, and said, "See? This is the way you do at sea, just lie down in your bunk and read."

Phillip reached up and took down a gas mask and a steel helmet from the top of his locker. "We're going to see action," he said, and put on the steel helmet.

Then I decided it was about time to find the chief mate and give him our job slips, so I told Phil to wait for me and went first to the mess. Some navy gunners were sitting there drinking coffee and playing cards.

"Where'd this ship go last trip?" I asked.

One of them, a husky blond sailor in shorts, said, "Italy. This time France, I think."

I went topside to the mate's stateroom. No one was there, so I went back to my fo'c'sle and stretched out on my bunk again. Then it occurred to me for the first time that Phil had laid Barbara last night.

"Say," I said, "you finally did it last night, didn't you?" I started to applaud, clapping my hands. Phil had dug out some books from behind a locker and was throwing them away as he glanced at the titles.

"Tonight," I went on, "we'll go ashore and see our goils again."

At this point, a six-foot-four red-haired man wearing a dirty officer's cap and some old khaki stepped into our fo'c'sle.

"What's your names?" he yelled.

I told him.

"Did you sign on yet?"

"Are they signing on yet?" I asked innocently.

"Yeah, we're signing on."

"Well," I said, "the bosun . . . and the other guys
. . . told us to wait until later . . . or—"

"Yeah?" said the red-haired giant. I began to realize that he was probably the bastard chief mate.

"Get off the ship," he said.

"Why?"

"Ask me once more," he said, "and I'll throw you
off myself."

"Well—"

"Never mind!" he shouted. "Who do you guys think
you are, anyway? You come on a ship, you sign on. If
you don't want to sign, get off."

"The bosun—" I began.

"Never mind the bosun!" he yelled. "Get off the
ship. And you ought to drop a couple of quarters in the
kitty for using that water for showers."

I sat up indecisively.

"Did you hear what I said? Get off!" he shouted. "I
don't want anybody in my crew that won't cooperate."

"Are you the chief mate?"

"Yeah, I'm the chief mate."

"Well," I said, "what about the rest of the deck
crew? I was led to understand that—"

"Never mind that. Get off now!"

I said, "All right, don't get your water hot," and started to pick up my shirt. Phil was standing in the corner of the fo'c'sle, looking at the mate. The mate scowled awhile at me and then left.

I jumped up from my bunk and went over to the locker and took out my gear. "Get your stuff," I said. "We're not staying on this damned ship." I took my two canvas bags out of the locker and slammed them on the deck. Then I rushed down the alleyway to the officers' mess.

They had the shipping articles laid out on tables in there, and there were several officers, some seamen signing on, and the shipping commissioner puffing on his pipe.

"What about Ryko and Tourian?" the shipping commissioner barked at me when I told him our names. "Is that you?"

"Yes," I said. "What's the story?"

"There's no story. The chief's ordered you two off the crew list." With this the commissioner turned his head away.

I went back to the fo'c'sle, picked up my bags, and stepped out in the alleyway. "Fuck you all!" I hollered down the alleyway, and started for the gangplank with Phil at my heels.

The bosun was standing in front of the gangplank. "Gettin' off?" he asked.

"What the hell," I said. "You told us to wait. What's going on around here?"

The bosun looked at me a little blankly. He didn't seem to know what it was all about, and evidently he didn't even know that he had started it all himself.

"Are you signed on?" I finally asked him.

"I just did," he said.

That was the payoff. I walked down the gangplank with Phillip.

The bosun followed us down. "Listen," he told us on the dock, "you guys want to sign on and they won't let you? Okay. That means you go down to the beef window at the Union Hall and collect a month's pay from this company, see? Union rules say a seaman can't be turned away once he's assigned to a ship. Do you follow me?"

"Yeah," I said, a little wearily.

And he went on to tell us everything about the union rules, and the month's pay we had coming by rights, and how we should beef and beef, and how the mate had nothing on us.

In the end, I asked him to give us a dime so we could get home and he handed me a quarter, saying, "Don't let that prick of a chief mate put anything over on you."

So Phil and I started to walk back across the dock. Longshoremen were loading on some U.S. Army tanks on a freighter across the way, and outside the shed a freight train was puffing in, hauling a string of flatcars carrying tanks, jeeps, and trucks. In the slip a barge was docked, alongside another Liberty ship, and a tremendous crane was hauling up 20mm antiaircraft guns to the platform on the flying bridge of the ship.

Phil and I watched some of this for a while, then we picked up our bags and left.

It was still hot and sunny, so we stopped halfway up Montague Street to buy a quart of orange soda in a variety store. We sat on our sea bags outside the store and drank the soda, which was lukewarm and sweet.

"Don't worry," I said to Phil, who looked disconsolate. "Monday we'll go to the beef window at the hall and get another ship."

He didn't say anything, so I went back into the store and cashed in the bottle, and then we walked to the subway at Borough Hall.

14

WILL DENNISON

By Saturday I was tired of being a detective. The boss was an all-around heel and he kept encroaching on my leisure time with errands to do on the way home that turned out to be at the other end of town from where I live and took hours to do.

I got to Al's about eight o'clock after one of these errands which involved a trip to the Bronx. We decided to go down to Washington Square and wish the sailors bon voyage.

When we walked into Apartment 32 I saw Barbara and Phillip lying on the couch. Phillip had nothing on but his khaki merchant marine pants, and Barbara was in her slip. They just lay there without moving. Phillip looked up at Al sullenly and moved a little closer to Barbara.

I walked past them into the other room. Mike and Janie were in the bedroom. Mike put on a pair of khaki pants and came out and said hello.

I sat down and said, "What time do you boys ship out in the morning?"

Mike said, "We're not shipping out. We got fired."

I said, "Fired? I never heard of such a thing."

"Well that's what happened. When we got on the ship the bosun came up to us and advised us not to sign on because the chief mate was a bastard. Well, we went downstairs, drank some milk, took a shower, and pretty soon the mate came down. Great big bastard, six-foot-four and red-haired. He says, 'I hear you boys can't decide whether to sign on or not. Get the fuck off this ship. I ought to charge you for taking a shower.' So we were fired."

Janie came out of the bedroom. She said, "I knew they wouldn't leave."

Mike said, "We'll ship out Monday for sure."

Janie said, "Yes you will."

I sighed and said, "Have you people eaten yet?"

They all said no, and there was one of those discussions should we go out to eat or bring food back to the apartment. Janie said, "Let's go out. I'm sick of sitting around this apartment. We've been here all day."

Everyone began putting on clothes.

We walked over to a lunch counter on Sixth Avenue. I ordered some ice cream, since I had eaten an early lunch. Then I changed my mind and ordered a stuffed pepper. They both arrived together. The pepper was pretty bad.

Phillip sat down next to me at the counter, as far as possible from Al, who was at the other end of the counter.

After this terrible food, for which I paid since no one else had any money, we walked out onto Sixth Avenue and stood on the sidewalk by a high wire fence that ran around an apartment-house park. Al climbed over the fence and lay down in the weeds on the other side. Barbara sat on a bench and Phillip lay down with his head in her lap. People walked by in the hot night.

I was talking to Mike about the merchant marine and asked him why he didn't wear a uniform around, to get all the free handouts.

He said, "It seems like a finkish thing to do."

I said, "This is a finkish world."

There was talk about going to see *La Grand Illusion*, but Barbara said she had seen it five times and knew just what Erich von Stroheim was going to do all the time.

The head-in-lap act had broken up and the young couple were on their feet now. Phillip was talking about his father. I heard him say: "The old man should be out in a couple of years now."

We decided to go across the street for some beer. Climbing back over the fence, Al slipped and fell heavily to the sidewalk. I helped him up and said, "Are you hurt?"

He said, "I think I twisted my ankle."

Phillip and Barbara were already halfway across the street. We all went into a bar and sat at a table in the back. Al was limping.

There was a silly drunk dancing around in front of the jukebox, so we had one round, then Janie said, "Let's go to the Germania and get some good beer." So we paid and left.

I walked ahead with Phillip and Barbara. I asked Phillip when he was going to get a ship, and he said Monday. Then we talked about Rimbaud. Barbara walked along not saying anything. I thought she was sulking. Al was limping busily along, about ten feet to the rear, but Phillip paid him no attention.

We went into the Germania. Before the war this was one of the noisiest and most disagreeable places in the whole of New York City. There used to be young people sitting around in large clusters singing college songs, and fights kept breaking out in the men's room where drunken college boys suffered from delusions of homosexual persecution. Now there was nothing to distinguish it from any other place.

We sat at a long wood table and ordered beer, which arrived in large steins. Phillip sat opposite Barbara and he stuck his head across the table from time to time and she petted him on the hair. It was disgusting. Finally he leaned over and took her right index finger in his teeth. The nail makeup was a little loose and he peeled it off with his teeth.

Mike repeated the story about how the mate threw them off the ship. Janie belched, and everyone else was yawning or cleaning their nails or looking around.

Finally Barbara said she had to catch a train back to Manhasset, and Phillip got up to go with her to the subway. Al looked at him imploringly, like a dog that wants to accompany its master. Phillip walked away without looking at him.

Mike was telling about the sinking of the S.S. *American Star*, a troopship, in the North Atlantic. He'd heard this story from a survivor, one night in a bar in Chicago.

"It was a terrible thing," the survivor had said. "It was all dark and you couldn't see anything. I was on a life raft with a nigger cook, and all around me I could hear those drowning soldiers calling for their mothers."

15

WILL DENNISON

SUNDAY I DID NOT SEE AL UNTIL AROUND SIX o'clock, when I was ready for dinner. The fact is, I was not in a hurry to hear the events of Saturday evening gone over piece by piece.

Al was asleep when I knocked at his door. He said to come in. I found him lying on the bed, covered with a light blanket. The shades were drawn and the room was dark. I asked him if he was ready for dinner and he said yes. Then he closed his eyes. I sat down and turned on the light and glanced through a copy of the *New Yorker* that had been on the floor.

Al pushed the blanket aside and swung his legs to the floor. He was completely dressed, except for his shoes. He yawned and smiled. Then he walked over to the washbasin, dabbed some water on his face, and combed his hair.

I was reading a short story in the *New Yorker*. Something about two women in Schrafft's.

Al put on a pair of cracked shoes and we went out to buy some food. We bought some hard rolls, sliced ham, cheese, apples, and milk in a delicatessen on Sixth Avenue. Then we walked back to Al's room and started to eat.

Al said, "You know, Dennison, there's something vampirish about that girl."

"Barbara? Yeah. Do you notice how red her lips are and how pale her skin? Fah! 'Tis unnatural."

Al said, "When I came into the room and saw them lying there on the couch, I had the feeling she was sucking all the life out of him."

"There certainly isn't much sex in that affair," I said. "It gives me the horrors."

"He looks pale. He doesn't look well at all."

We ate for a while in silence, and I was getting ready to hear Al say why did Phillip have to get involved with all these women when he obviously wasn't in love with them and why couldn't Phillip love him, or maybe he did already in which case he ought to show it. Al did say all that, and I went on eating.

Al continued. "I wonder if I should ship out anyway. Perhaps when he found out I was on the ship he would be glad."

I said, "I don't know. Do what you like. My advice is to stay here and make yourself some money. He'll be back in five or six weeks. If you can build up a marijuana business while he's away, you'll have something to offer him."

Al said, "I don't see why money should be so important."

I didn't want to go into that again, so I didn't say anything, and Al said he would definitely go down the following morning to get some marijuana seed.

We finished dinner and Al said he was going down to Washington Square. He asked me did I want to come along and I said, "No, I was just there last night."

We said good night on 52nd Street and Al walked away toward Fifth Avenue to take the bus. I walked over to Broadway, took the IRT down to Sheridan Square, and went home.

About ten o'clock Danny Borman called and asked could he come right over. I said yes.

When I opened the door, he slid in like a jittery gangster who is in wrong with the mob. He threw down a shot of whiskey and started telling what happened last night.

He had been in a bar and some merchant seaman flashed a big roll. Danny got acquainted, and they went back to this guy's apartment to get a bottle. When they got there the seaman began telling Danny he would still be in the army except he was discharged for wounds he got in the Pacific. Danny said, "Yeah, sure." The seaman said, "Oh, you don't believe I was in the army? I'll show you I was in the army. I got my discharge right here." He turned around and began rummaging through a bureau drawer. So then Danny k-norcked him with the sap. The guy's head was so hard he just shook his head and started hollering. Danny started for the door, and by this time everybody was out on the landing to see what was going on. Danny jumped out of a window on the landing, this being the second floor, and made his escape, as they say in the newspapers. But he threw away the sap.

He sat there twisting an empty jigger in his hand, looking nervous and discouraged.

I said, "Danny, would you be interested in burning down a house for two hundred dollars?"

His face brightened up and he said, "That sounds pretty good."

So I told him about a shipyard worker I knew who figured he had got a dirty deal from some girl and her old lady and wanted to burn down their house but couldn't do it because he would be suspected. He was willing to pay two hundred to have it done, this being a wood house in Long Island somewhere.

Danny asked, "Does she have to be in it? If so, I don't want the job. Two hundred isn't enough to burn a live broad, no matter what she done."

I told him no, she wasn't going to be at home, and the guy would tell him when she would be out.

Danny said, "It's a cinch."

So I said, "Wait a minute," and I rang the guy's number, but he wasn't in. I gave Danny the number and told him to call again later. "Just say Will recommended you for that house repair job. I told him if I found someone I'd have him get in touch."

Danny thanked me and wrote the number down. He said when he got the money he'd fix me up.

I rubbed my hands and said, "Whatever you think is fair. The job is easy, but it's not in my line." (My line is letting other people take the risks, like Phillip's old man.)

"I'm sure this guy's all right," I went on, "and I know where he lives. There won't be any trouble collecting, but get half on account."

Danny said, "You know me, Will." He got up to go. "Say, I'm sorry about the sap."

I said, "Why, that's all right. I'm glad you didn't get yourself in a jam."

16

WILL DENNISON

IT WAS ABOUT SEVEN O'CLOCK MONDAY MORNING
when my buzzer rang and woke me up. I put on my
shorts and went out into the other room and pressed
the button to release the outer door.

I said, "Who's there?"

"It's me."

It was Phillip's voice, and I opened the door and
Phillip slid in quick.

"Here," he said, "have the last cigarette."

He held out a pack of Lucky Strikes smeared with
blood. There was one cigarette left in the pack.

"I just killed Al and threw the body off a warehouse."

I took the cigarette and held it in my hand.

Then I went and sat on the couch and motioned
him to a chair opposite me. I said, "Sit down and tell
me all about it."

He sat down and said, "I need a hundred dollars to skip the country. I'm going to Mexico."

I said, "Not so fast, young man. What's all this about Al."

"Well," he said, "Al and I were drinking in Minetta's, and we decided to take a walk. We walked over on Second Avenue somewhere and broke into an old warehouse and started exploring around. I found a hatchet and broke some windows with it.

"Later we were up on the roof. Al kept saying he wanted to ship out with me. I got mad and gave him a shove. He nearly went over. He looked at me and said, 'I want to do the things you do. I want to write poetry and go to sea and all that.'" Phillip stopped and looked at me. "I can see you don't believe me."

"Go on," I said.

"Well, so I said to him, 'Do you want to die?' and he said, 'Yes.' He made a couple of wisecracks and tried to put his arm around me. I still had the hatchet in my hand, so I hit him on the forehead. He fell down. He was dead. Now give me that hundred dollars. I have to get out of the country."

"That's ridiculous. You can't skip the country with a hundred dollars."

"Yes I can. I'm going to hitchhike."

"Well, you'd get picked up quick enough."

"You don't believe me?" he said. "You know, don't you, that things drag on for just so long and then something happens."

I said, "All right, Al is dead now. What did you do then?"

"Well, then he kept leering at me through half-closed eyes. I said to him, 'You can't do that, you're dead.' I rolled him off the roof with my foot. It was about seven stories high."

"Anybody see you?"

"No, I don't think so."

"But you were seen leaving Minetta's together." I was thinking fast, and it all added up to one thing.

"Now give me that hundred dollars or I'll kill you too."

I smiled at him.

Phillip said, "Oh no, I wouldn't do that, but please let me have it."

I didn't answer.

He took a bloody silk handkerchief out of his pocket. In one corner there were the initials, "R.A." He stuck it under my nose.

"You recognize this don't you?"

"Yes," I said, "that's Al's. Souvenir, eh?"

He looked at me with a naive, boyish expression, and pushed the handkerchief toward me.

"Do you want this? Shall I leave it here?"

"Christ, no! Take it with you."

I put on my dressing gown and began pacing the room.

Phillip said, "What am I going to do if you won't give me any money? I'll get the hot seat."

I put on my Claude Rains manner and walked over toward him. "The hot seat," I sneered. "You'll be out in two years at the latest."

"Do you know what happened to you, Phil? You were attacked. Al attacked you. He tried to rape you. You lost your head. Everything went black. You hit him. He stumbled back and fell off the roof. You were in a panic. Your only thought was to get away. Get a good lawyer, you'll be out in two years."

Phil looked at me and nodded. "Well," he said, "I guess I could stand two years. But I don't know. Would you lend me your gun? I'll commit suicide. You do have a gun, don't you?"

I said, "Yes, I have a gun."

"But you don't have any bullets, do you?"

He knew damned well I had bullets. I said, "No, I haven't any bullets."

Phillip got up to leave and walked over to the door. I walked over and stood beside him. I thought that if it was true, I ought to put my hand on his shoulder and say something kind to cheer him up. But then I remembered how he was always trying to get money out of me.

I said, "Good-bye, Phillip," coldly.

He said good-bye and walked out.

I closed the door. Then I picked up the bloody pack of cigarettes off the floor, tore it up into small pieces, dropped the pieces into the toilet bowl, and flushed the toilet.

It was time to go to work, so I started to get dressed.

17

MIKE RYKO

MONDAY MORNING AT NINE O'CLOCK I WAS UP AND
ready to go to the Union Hall to get another ship, but
Phillip was nowhere around. I looked behind the couch
and saw that his sea bag was still there. So I sat down
and waited, figuring he might have gone downstairs
to get breakfast and would come back to get me. I sat
and lit a cigarette and started thinking about what we
would have to say at the beef window in order to get
another ship today.

The buzzer rang three times, which is the signal
for telephone calls, so I went downstairs to the lobby
and picked up the receiver.

"Hello," I said.

"Mike, this is Phil."

It was the first time I'd ever heard Phil's voice over
the phone, and I smiled because it sounded strange.

He said, "I disposed of the old man last night."

I said, "What?" and then for some reason I knew what he meant, right away.

"Where are you?" I asked.

He said he was at the Anchor Bar.

"What are you doing there?"

"I don't know," he said. "Come on over."

"Right away," I said, and hung up.

There was a woman entering the lobby carrying two shopping bags, and she was having difficulty opening the door. I watched her until she got the door opened, then I went back upstairs.

I reached behind the couch and hauled out Phillip's sea bag. I went to the bedroom and found the cat sleeping on my sea bags. I picked up the cat and laid it on the bed beside Janie. She was sleeping, and there was a thin film of moisture on her face. It was already hot at nine o'clock.

I picked up my sea bags and threw them beside Phillip's sea bag on the floor of the front room. I stood there looking at them for a minute or so. I couldn't think.

Then I decided it was useless to take them along, because now neither one of us could ship out. So I left the apartment and walked down the stairs.

When I got down to the lobby, I suddenly turned around and went back up the stairs on the run, went to the bedroom, kneeled at the bed, and kissed Janie on the brow.

I said, "I'll be back tonight," and she mumbled something and went back to sleep. Then I left the apartment house and walked rapidly toward the Union Hall.

The sun was hot and moist and you could already feel the heat breathing all round. I was sore because it was going to be a hot day. An old woman at the corner of 14th Street and Seventh Avenue tried to sell me some flowers but I rushed right by her.

When I got to the Anchor Bar, Phillip was standing at the bar with a whiskey glass half empty in his hand and several dollars and some change laid out in front of him on the counter. The place was full of seamen all talking at the same time and the jukebox was playing some South American record.

We said hello and Phillip ordered me a drink. I fixed my eyes on a ceiling fan above and let the whiskey slide into my mouth, then I took a beer.

I looked at Phillip and said, "So you disposed of the old man last night. Where is he?"

"In a warehouse yard."

"Dead?"

"Of course."

I looked at Phillip closely. I said, "Well, well," and he leered at me, smiling.

Then he pulled out a handkerchief from his pocket and showed it to me. There were some red stains on it, and the initials "R.A." embroidered in a corner.

"Al's?" I asked.

He nodded his head. Then he pointed down to the cuffs of his khaki pants and held up his foot. There were some red stains there, too. "Blood," he said.

I didn't know whether to believe all this or not, because he was so anxious to show me the evidence.

"How did you do it?" I asked.

"With a hatchet. I hit him on the brow and he fell down dead. Then I pushed him over the edge of the roof." Phillip put his hands over his ears and pressed hard. "I did this for three seconds so I wouldn't hear him fall in the yard." He winced and made a face. "I heard it nonetheless."

"Tell me all about it," I said. My legs kept bending at the knee and I had to lean most of my weight on the bar. I said, "Let's go somewhere and sit. My knees are shaky, I can't stand up."

"Me too," he said, and picked up his money and cigarettes from the counter.

We walked out of the Anchor Bar, crossed the street, and started up 17th Street. In a play court on the right, a whole platoon of little children were seesawing and playing hopscotch and wading in a pool in the hot sun. Phillip smiled at the children. I knew he was thinking of himself as a murderer.

We walked uptown along Eighth Avenue, and I gave one last glance at the group of seamen standing around in front of the Union Hall.

We found an air-conditioned bar a few blocks up the avenue. There were some red leather stools at the bar there, so we sat on them and ordered a couple of Calvert shots with beer chasers.

"Tell me what else happened," I said. "Tell me everything since I last saw you, yesterday morning."

"I spent all Sunday afternoon at my uncle's," Phillip said. "I told him I needed some more money because we had to get another ship. After dinner I went down to Minetta's and started drinking whiskey, and then Al came in with Cathcart. Cathcart went home early and Al and I drank some more whiskey."

So then Phillip gave me the story he'd told Dennison earlier in the morning. When he was finished I said, "What are you going to do?"

"Any suggestions?"

"Substantially what Dennison advised."

"I guess that's best," Phillip said, and ordered two more drinks. "I'll get the hot seat for sure."

"No," I said. "That's preposterous. Al was queer. He chased you over continents. He screwed up your life. The police will understand that."

Phillip shrugged.

And then I said, "Well at least we'll have a good drunk this morning." I was sorry I said that, so I said, "But God, it shouldn't have happened, huh?"

Phillip shrugged again.

"Here's to Al anyway," I added, and held up my glass.

I drank down my Calvert and the next thing I knew Phillip was staring into space and two long tears were running down his cheeks. I was all embarrassed, because I had never seen Phillip cry. I wanted to put my hand on his shoulder, and finally I did.

"'There's time for all kinds of things,'" I said, "'time even for murder.' Saroyan."

He leered at me, his face all wet. "That sounds like T. S. Eliot," he said.

"Does it?"

We laughed a little bit, and then I gave him a cigarette. I began to think about how I used to imagine what it would be like to kill someone and how I used to write thousands of words to create that pattern of emotions. Now here stood Phillip beside me, and he had actually done it.

"I'm going to my uncle's and give myself up," Phillip was saying. "He'll know what to do, he'll get lawyers. If the police haven't found Al's body by now, they will have, before nightfall."

I explained to Phillip what I was thinking about, but he was concerned with facts.

"My uncle has a lot of political power," he went on, "and he'll know just what lawyers to get."

We talked about that for a while, then Phillip said he wanted to go.

"Where are you going?" I asked.

"Let's go to the Museum of Modern Art and spend a few hours there."

"Okay," I said, "but let's have a few drinks before we go in."

We went outside on Eighth Avenue to hail a cab. The sidewalks were crowded with people. A fruit vendor had pulled his cart up in front of the bar and was selling apples. We finally stopped a cab and jumped in.

"Go by way of Times Square," Phillip said. Then, when the cab was under way, he turned to me and said in a loud voice, "I hope they don't find the body right away."

"Yeah," I said loudly, and we were grinning at each other. "I'll bet he's a bloody mess."

"Hell, yes," Phillip said. "When I chopped him in

the face with the hatchet, the blood spurted out and gushed all over the roof. There must be a lot more blood down in the yard."

"Yes," I said, "you did a thorough job of it."

We were passing through Times Square and Phillip said, "Drop us off here, driver."

The cabby pulled up to the curb and turned to close the meter. Phillip handed him the money, and the cabby was grinning. The cabby knew the ropes, all right, but he didn't know the facts.

On the sidewalk I said, "I thought we were going to the museum."

"Let's look around here awhile," Phillip said, and started walking down 42nd Street.

We passed the Apollo theater, which was still playing *Port of Shadows,* and the Italian spaghetti joint, and then we crossed the street to a penny arcade.

Phillip cashed in a quarter's worth of pennies, and we started playing pinball machines and shooting down enemy aircraft and looking at the risqué penny movies that depicted women undressing in their boudoirs while mustached men came in from the fire escape. I shoved a nickel in the jukebox and played Benny Goodman's "The World Is Waiting for the Sunrise."

We left the penny arcade and wandered toward Sixth Avenue. Phil bought some roasted peanuts from a little Italian and we sat in the New York Public Library park, throwing peanuts at the pigeons. A man in shirtsleeves sat next to us on the bench, reading a Trotskyite pamphlet.

Phil said, "Wherever they send me, I'll be able to do what I would have done at sea."

"You know," I said, "I knew we wouldn't ship out, because I wasn't dreaming about the sea."

"I'll write poetry," Phillip said.

There was a movie house on 42nd Street near Sixth Avenue showing Alexander Korda's production of *Four Feathers*.

Phillip said, "That's good. Let's go in and see it." So we went in and sat in an orchestra seat. Something had gone wrong with the air-conditioning system and it was suffocating in there.

The picture started off with a caption telling of the murder of thousands of British soldiers in the Sudan at the hands of the ruthless Fuzzy Wuzzies. Phillip waved his hand and said, "*They* can murder 'em by the thousands."

"Yeah," I said.

There was an ambush scene where you saw British soldiers and Fuzzy Wuzzies hacking away at each other with sabers and knives and much blood. Most of the picture kept reminding us of Al lying in the yard in a pool of blood, so we couldn't enjoy it that much. And one of the characters in the story was named Dennison.

We came out of the theater soaking wet with sweat, and it was even hotter outside. It was now about three-thirty. We went into a bar and drank a few glasses of cold beer.

"I'll have to go soon," Phillip said.

I said, "What about the museum?"

"That was a good picture," Phillip said, "but it kept reminding me that my time is drawing near."

We drank and were silent.

"Well," he said at length, "let's go to the museum."

We went out and hailed a cab.

In the air-cooled museum Phil spent ten minutes in front of a portrait of Jean Cocteau by Modigliani. I wandered off to look at Blume's vast studies of the decline and fall of the West, with Corinthian pillars fallen and always the same underworld types plotting in cellars while priests wail at the sacrifice and Oriental-looking troops gut the city. Then we both stopped in front of Tchelitchew's *Cache-Cache* and looked at that for a while.

There was a tall blond fag, wearing a striped polo shirt and tan slacks, who kept looking at Phil out of the corner of his eye. Even when we went downstairs to see the one-hour movie, the fag was sitting just behind us.

The movie was an old Italian film made in 1915 with Eleonora Duse in it. Phillip and I thought she was great. There was something virile in her attitude toward tragedy, as though she were defying God to knock off the chip He Himself had placed on her shoulder.

We went back upstairs to the paintings. I wanted to drink some beer but Phillip insisted on staying in the museum till closing time. I looked around to see if the fag was still tailing Phil, but I didn't see him.

Phillip again installed himself in front of Modigliani's portrait and kept looking at it, with a smile on his face.

I said, "Meet me down in the bar on 53rd Street. I'm thirsty."

Phillip said, "All right," and I went out of the museum. The blond fag was talking to a young man in the lobby.

In the bar I took a table in the corner and ordered a bottle of Schlitz beer. The waiter brought it and set it down on the white tablecloth. He didn't like the way I was dressed, and his manner was a bit indulgent. I was wondering why people made such a fuss over clothes, and while I was thinking about these things the idea of the murder kept popping up and down in a steady rhythm.

I got hungry after a while, so I ordered a hamburger steak dinner. The waiter brought over silverware and a clean white napkin and a glass of water. The place had that brown east-side light in it, like a rathskeller, and it was cool and pleasant. I looked around, and took in all the characters that were in there.

While I was waiting for the hamburger steak, I ordered a double bourbon and drank it down in two gulps. When the food came, I ate loosely and goofily, the way you do when you've had too many martinis before dinner.

I was finished and was drinking some beer when Phillip walked in and looked around. I waved at him and he came over.

"I ate," I said, "I was hungry."

"Don't apologize, ghoul. I'm hungry too."

"Okay," I said.

Phillip ordered the same dinner plus a bottle of beer, and I ordered another double bourbon.

The waiter was beginning to brighten up to his table. He was beginning to say "Sir," and before you knew it he had emptied out my ashtray and wiped it clean with a moist towel.

Phillip said, "I've got about ten dollars left of my uncle's money. We might as well spend it all before I give myself up."

"Fine," I said.

Phillip finished eating, and paid the check. We went out on 53rd Street and wandered east until we got to Third Avenue. We found a cheap saloon and went in and sat at the bar.

"This is where Don Birnam does all his drinking in *The Lost Weekend*," I said. "Third Avenue."

Phillip ordered two whiskeys and we were launched off again. The door of the bar was open, and a cool late afternoon breeze was blowing in.

Phillip was getting very nervous now. He kept saying he'd have to go home soon, and I kept reminding him of Boldieu and his white gloves in *La Grand Illusion*.

Two soldiers were sitting next to us. They looked like they had spent a winter in the North African campaign. One of them was looking at me and finally he leaned over and wanted to know if there were any whorehouses in this town.

I wrote down an address for him. "I'm not sure they're still operating," I said, "but try it anyway."

The other soldier started talking to Phillip and asked him how he liked the merchant marine.

Phillip said it was fine, and a minute later he got up and stuck out his hand to me.

"Well, Mike, so long."

He took me by surprise. "So long," I said.

Phillip walked out the door and I followed him, leaving my change and cigarettes on the bar.

We stopped outside the door. Phillip stuck out his hand again. He had some change in it. When we shook hands the coins jingled and a few of them dropped down on the sidewalk and clinked. Phillip opened his hand and let the rest of the money drop down from stiff, dramatic fingers.

"I'll pick them up," I warned him.

"Go ahead. So long, Mike."

"So long, Phil."

Phillip walked away toward 60th Street and I watched him for a while. I felt like running after him to say good-bye again. He disappeared around the corner walking determinedly, as if he were on his way to work, and I went back inside the bar. I saw the change on the sidewalk and went back outside to pick it up. Then I reentered the bar and ordered a beer and sat in an empty booth.

It was the loneliest beer I ever had.

I finally walked out and there I was, all alone, standing on Third Avenue in the late afternoon. The Elevated roared by overhead, and the big trucks rumbled by. Here I was, all alone, and everything was finished.

I decided right then and there to go off and travel again. I felt like seeing the Pennsylvania hills again, and the scrub pines of North Carolina. I was standing there thinking about this when I saw Phillip returning down Third Avenue, running.

"What's the matter?" I was running toward him.

He took the bloody handkerchief from his pocket and handed it to me.

"What'll I do with this?" he asked. "Want it?"

"Why?"

"It's Al's handkerchief."

"I know."

"We've got to get rid of it," he said.

"That's easy," I said. I took the handkerchief and dropped it in the gutter. Then we started laughing.

We were both nervous and half crazy, glad to see each other again.

"Let's go into a bar," I said.

"Okay," he said.

We went to another saloon on Third Avenue and started drinking again. The bar was full of Third Avenue characters, and the bartender was fat and Irish.

"I gotta go home," Phillip kept saying. Then he said, "I'm getting sick of my white gloves." He held up his hands. "I'm weak. The gloves are beginning to chafe."

I felt so lousy I didn't say anything. We were just beginning to realize what had happened.

"I'll walk you home," I told him.

We had another drink or two and then we were out on the street. I kept saying, "Well . . ." and Phillip kept saying, "Well . . ." also, and both of us had a lot to say, but there was no room to say it in, we were so tense and close.

We finally reached Central Park South, and there was Phillip's uncle's apartment house. We walked up to the entrance and stopped.

Phillip waved at the doorman and then said to me, "He's a neurotic. Some guy."

I said, "Yeah."

We paused and automatically stuck out our hands.

"Well," said Phillip, "here we go again. See you behind bars."

"I'll go and see you," I said.

"Bring me good books and all that."

"Yeah."

We shook hands and patted each other on the shoulders and leered at each other, smiling. Then he said "So long" and I said "So long" and he turned and went into the lobby, and I walked toward Columbus Circle where two big trucks went by that made me want to travel far.

18

WILL DENNISON

PHILLIP'S UNCLE FIXED EVERYTHING UP AND HAD the boy committed to the state nuthouse. I figure he won't be there more than six months because the uncle knows several doctors on the board who will play ball.

The cops weren't too pleased about the way I knew about the murder and still didn't rush to the nearest phone like a decent citizen who are all supposed to be stool pigeons according to the official ruling. Anyway, I don't like any sort of publicity. So I took a trip out to Chicago for a few weeks to renew some old acquaintances.

That town isn't what it was. Seems like everybody I used to know there five years ago is either dead, in jail, or in the army. But I ran into a few guys I used to know who were still hanging out in the old spots, around North and Halsted.

When I got back to New York there was a letter from a man in Chicago saying he was a friend of Charley Anderson and would like to see me about a business proposition. There would be something in it for me. It sounded like he had some hot stuff and didn't know where to take it. There was a phone number in the letter and I called it several times, but did not get the party.

I decided to go up to Al's place and see Agnes, who had moved into Al's room after the murder. I found her packing. She was going to leave town the next day.

It seemed a Mrs. Rogers had bought the house from Mrs. Frascati and she was weeding out the disorderly elements. Chris Rivers had been thrown out as a chronic deadbeat and sanitary problem. "She's going to redecorate and raise the rents," Agnes told me.

"What happened to Hugh Maddox?" I asked.

"He got three years, but may be allowed to join the army later. No one seems to know for certain."

We thought that over for a while, then Agnes said, "Oh, and another thing. You know I packed Al's things and sent them off to his brother in Memphis. But the radio was missing. Someone must have gone into the room and taken it. I think it was Bunny, that socialite thief from Boston."

I said, "Very likely."

We sat there in Al's old room and it began to get dark. Agnes was telling a long story about Mrs. Rogers, but I didn't listen. Finally I got up to go.

"If you get out West, look up my old lady," I told her. "Just ask anybody where is Mrs. Dennison's grocery store."

Agnes said she would do it if she got out to Reno, then we shook hands and said good-bye at the door.

I went to the Three G's alone and ate dinner.

As I was walking home from Sheridan Square someone stepped out of a doorway and said, "Hello, Will." It was Danny Borman.

I said, "Well Danny, how are things going, like a house afire, hey?" but he didn't think that was funny.

We went back to my room and he began telling me what had happened.

He did set fire to the house, and several other houses caught fire, which wouldn't have amounted to much except that some unpatriotic prick had a lot of gasoline hoarded in his basement. Anyway the fire got so big it set fire to a defense plant and a wing of the plant burned down. Somebody yelled sabotage and the FBI was on the case.

I asked Danny if he collected, and he said yes. He was going to blow town with the money. I didn't have the heart to ask him for a cut, and he didn't try to force it on me.

So we said good-bye and good luck and so forth. Then Danny asked me what had happened with Phillip, and I told him.

Danny thought about it for a minute and said, "Well, he can go into politics when he gets out."

"Yeah," I said. "He ought to be good at that."

THE END

AFTERWORD

Jack Kerouac was drinking and talking in his living room at 271 Sanders Avenue in his hometown of Lowell, Massachusetts, in October 1967. The young poets Ted Berrigan, Aram Saroyan, and Duncan McNaughton were sitting and talking with him; they had come to record an interview for *The Paris Review.* After a question about his first novel, *The Town and the City,* Kerouac remarked, "I also wrote another version [of that story] that's hidden under the floorboards, with Burroughs. It's called *And the Hippos Were Boiled in Their Tanks.*"

"Yes," said Berrigan, "I've heard rumors of that book. Everyone wants to get at that book."

As the exchange attests, *And the Hippos Were Boiled in Their Tanks* had already gained legendary status forty years ago. But when its two authors wrote the text in 1945 they were unpublished and unknown. *Hippos* predated by more than a decade the works that brought them lasting literary fame—*On the Road* in 1957 for Kerouac and *Naked Lunch* in 1959 for William S. Burroughs. Those books, along with Allen Ginsberg's *Howl and Other Poems* in 1956, are the flagship works of the Beat Generation and it seems unlikely that anyone reading this book will be entirely unaware of them.

Even if all you know about the *Hippos* novel comes from this book's jacket, you already know too much for you to meet the text as it was written, by two nobodies and about no one you ever heard of. Thanks to a virtual mountain of Beat bibliography, biography, belles lettres, memoirs, and new archival sources, most of the persons on whom Kerouac and Burroughs based their characters in 1945 are widely recognizable today. For better or worse, *Hippos* comes to you now as a "framed" work: *The Columbia murder that gave birth to the Beats! A lost Kerouac book! A lost Burroughs book!*

Today, sixty-odd years after it was composed, the setting of *Hippos*—New York City near the end of World War II—makes it a period piece. You'll want to bring to your reading of this text all the imagery you associate with that period, all the wartime music and automobiles and fashions, the movies and novels and headlines. But depending on which version of the "Lucien Carr–David Kammerer story" you have been served, you will probably want to throw out your preconceptions and let the novel's characters "Phillip Tourian" and "Ramsay Allen" speak for themselves.

For anyone who just walked in, the basics: the enmeshed relationship between Lucien Carr IV and David Eames Kammerer began in St. Louis, Missouri, in 1936, when Lucien was eleven and Dave was twenty-five. Eight years, five states, four prep schools, and two colleges later, that connection was grown too intense, those emotions too feverish; as "Will Dennison" writes in *Hippos*, "When they get together, something happens." Something had to give, and something finally did.

In the muggy predawn hours of Monday, August 14, 1944, in cruisy Riverside Park on New York's Upper West Side, Lucien and Dave were alone, drunk and quarreling. They wrestled and struggled in the grass, and then Lucien stabbed Dave with his little Boy Scout knife, twice, in the upper chest. Dave passed out. Lucien assumed he was dead and he rolled Dave's limp body into the Hudson River—unconscious and bleeding out, arms tied together with shoelaces, pants pockets weighted with rocks—to drown. It took Carr almost twenty-four hours to surrender himself to authorities and still another day for Dave to be hauled up at the foot of West 79th Street.

The killing was front-page news for a week in New York, but it was especially shocking to the three new friends whom Lucien had introduced to one another in his freshman year at Columbia University: Allen Ginsberg, eighteen, a fellow Columbia frosh from Paterson, New Jersey; Jack Kerouac, twenty-two, a recent Columbia dropout from Lowell; and William S. Burroughs, thirty, a Harvard graduate and Kammerer's friend since 1920, when they were school chums in St. Louis.

Today, many written explanations of the long, fraught relationship between Kammerer and Carr are available to the interested reader. In almost all of them, however, David is reduced to a pathetic caricature: the obsessive, older male homosexual stalker who increasingly oppresses his innocent, heterosexual victim, finally leaving the younger man no alternative but to "defend his honor" with violence. This was, in fact, the theory of Carr's legal defense, intended to be palatable to a judge, as well as to the public—especially in 1944.

There is much more to be said, however, about Lucien Carr's early life and youthful bisexuality than has ever been published in even the fullest, most reliable biographies of the major Beat figures. Lucien did, for example, share a number of sexual encounters with Ginsberg in 1944. So did Kammerer: that became clear when Ginsberg's early journals were published in 2006 as *The Book of Martyrdom and Artifice*. But Lucien

never had any sexual contact with Dave—not even
once, according to what Burroughs remembered Kammerer telling him often, and undoubtedly Dave would
have told his old friend Bill if anything at all had ever
happened.

To almost all who knew the actors, the retrospec-
tive sanitizing of Lucien's sexual history for public
consumption seemed forgivable, in the circumstances.
After all, even the dead man's oldest friend did not turn
against Carr. William Burroughs was the first person
to hear Lucien's confession, a few hours after the killing; he immediately suggested that Lucien get a good
lawyer and turn himself in, relying on the defense-of-
honor scenario. Burroughs felt that no purpose would
be served by Lucien taking the maximum fall.

When Lucien hurried to tell Jack the news next,
Kerouac was more ambivalent. He had found much to
like about David Kammerer. Jack's bisexuality was
confused and covert, but undeniable; he could not feel
any real contempt for Kammerer on that account. And
yet even though he and Carr had been friends for only
six months, Kerouac felt a loyalty to Lucien that over-
rode his misgivings.

They spent the day together, talking and drinking,
roving from bar to bar, looking at paintings, watching
art movies, and revisiting the places where all this

189

real-world drama had recently happened. Finally it was late afternoon, and the young men understood they had stalled as long as they could. Reluctantly, Jack and Lucien parted, each knowing that what had just occurred was going to change everything.

After spending most of August 14 with Kerouac, Lucien confessed to his mother, Marion Gratz Carr, in her apartment on 57th Street. She called her lawyer and Lucien told him the story. He took Lucien the next morning to the office of Frank S. Hogan, district attorney, to turn himself in. Carr was charged with second-degree murder and jailed. Kerouac was arrested at the apartment where he lived with his girlfriend, Edie Parker, no. 62, 421 West 118th Street; unable to pay his bail, he was held as a material witness.

When the police knocked on Burroughs's apartment door at 69 Bedford Street in Greenwich Village on Thursday morning, Bill was across town in the Lexington Hotel, working a divorce case for the William E. Shorten detective agency. He was to listen for "amorous noises" in the adjacent hotel room, where the target couple had made reservations—but they never checked in. As soon as Burroughs got word that he, too, was wanted as a witness, he contacted his parents in

St. Louis. They immediately arranged for him to re-
tain a good attorney, who walked his client in to the
DA's office for questioning and then walked him out,
free on bond.

Lucien's attorneys, Vincent J. Malone and Kenneth
Spence, offered the assistant DA Jacob Grumet their
client's guilty plea to a lesser charge, first-degree man-
slaughter. For the court and the press the lawyers had
painted the picture of an old queer harrassing a young
boy who was not at all homosexual—as Carr had perhaps seemed in the first news stories and photos from
jail, with his fair hair, boyish looks, and a volume of
Yeats's poetry clutched in his hand. The attorneys even
suggested that the much-larger Kammerer had physi-
cally menaced Lucien, but they did not want to try to
convince a jury that a vigorous nineteen-year-old was
incapable of defending himself with any measures
short of stabbing Dave in the heart . . . or running away,
for that matter.

Lucien was sentenced to the reformatory in Elmira,
New York, on September 15, 1944, to a maximum of
ten years' confinement. Ann Charters's biography of
Kerouac states that Carr's friends had expected him to
receive a suspended sentence, so they were shocked
when he was remanded to the corrections system. But
as Burroughs told Ted Morgan, "I was there in the

courtroom. . . . I walked out with Lucien's lawyer, who said [to me], 'I think it would have been very bad for his character, for him to get off scot free'—so his heart wasn't in the case at all, he didn't want to get him off. He was kind of moralistic about it." (That man may, however, have been right.)

Kerouac married Edie Parker while he was still in jail so that her family would bail him out. He went home with her to Grosse Pointe, Michigan, to work off his bond debt. That lasted only a few weeks. Jack headed back to New York in early October and entered his period of "Self-Ultimacy," as it is referred to in the biographies.

After Kammerer died Burroughs went to see Dr. Paul Federn, his psychiatrist at that time, every day for a week; then he went home to live with his parents in St. Louis for several weeks. Burroughs returned quietly to New York at the end of October and sublet an apartment at 360 Riverside Drive. Within a month Burroughs's underworld connections had introduced him to the effects of injecting morphine, and by December he was sharing this discovery with Allen and Jack.

For Burroughs, as we know, this was the beginning of a lifelong struggle with addiction and an endless series of habits and cures, back on, off again, until in 1980 he got on the methadone maintenance program.

* * *

Allen Ginsberg was among the first to try his hand at making literary hay with the Carr–Kammerer story: in late 1944 Allen wrote many notes and chapter drafts in his journals for a work that he considered calling "The Bloodsong." Ginsberg's now published journals include those writings, with many vivid scenes between him and Lucien and lively depictions of the Carr–Kammerer–Burroughs circle. Ginsberg's reconstruction of the ultimate encounter between Lucien and Dave that night is the most detailed, and possibly the most realistic, of all the dramatizations of Kammerer's final hours.

In November 1944, however, Ginsberg wrote in his journal: "Today the Dean called my novel 'smutty.'" The assistant dean of Columbia, Nicholas McKnight, had called Allen in for a talking-to after Harrison Ross Steeves, chair of the English department, tipped off McKnight to what his undergraduate was working on. Dean McKnight did not want more notoriety for Columbia from the case and he discouraged Ginsberg from continuing.

By fall 1944 Allen's friend the student poet John Hollander had already written a "Dostoyevskian" story about the killing for the *Columbia Spectator*, and the juicy details proved irresistible to many other writers in those years. Some version of the affair turns up in novels and memoirs written in the 1940s, or later, by Chandler Brossard, William Gaddis, Alan Harrington, John Clellon Holmes, Anatole Broyard, Howard Mitcham, and even James Baldwin—who is believed to have used the characters for a story he called "Ignorant Armies," a very early version of his gay-themed 1956 novel *Giovanni's Room.*

Other New York writers who were certainly aware of the story include Kammerer's (and Brossard's) friend Marguerite Young and a friend of hers, a copyboy at *The New Yorker* named Truman Capote, to whom Young introduced Burroughs around June 1945, when Capote's first important story, "Miriam," was published in *Mademoiselle.* Years later Edie Kerouac Parker, another eyewitness, wrote her memoirs; her story was finally published in 2007 as *You'll Be Okay: My Life with Jack Kerouac.* Edie's account is from the perspective of Jack's girlfriend, who didn't immediately understand why the police banged on her apartment door and took her man away to jail.

And then there were Burroughs and Kerouac. William spoke at length to his first biographer, Ted Morgan, in the mid-1980s for Morgan's indispensable *Literary Outlaw: The Life and Times of William S. Burroughs.*

"Kerouac and I were talking about a possible book that we might write together, and we decided to do Dave's death. We wrote alternate chapters and read them to each other. There was a clear separation of material as to who wrote what. We weren't trying for literal accuracy at all, [just] some approximation. We had fun doing it.

"Of course, [what we wrote] was dictated by the actual course of events—that is, [Jack] knew one thing, and I knew another. We fictionalized. [The killing] was actually done with a knife, it wasn't done with a hatchet at all. I had to disguise the characters, so I made [Lucien's character] a Turk.

"Kerouac hadn't published anything [yet], we were completely unknown to anybody. At any rate, no one was interested in publishing it. We went to some agent [Madeline Brennan, of Ingersoll & Brennan] and she said, 'Oh yes, you're *talented*. You're *writers!*' and all this kind of stuff. But nothing came of it, no publisher was interested.

"And in hindsight, I don't see why they should have been. It had no commercial possibilities. It wasn't sensational enough to make it [...] from that point of view, nor was it well-written or interesting enough to make it [from] a purely literary point of view. It sort of fell in-between. [It was] very much in the Existentialist genre,

195

the prevailing mode of the period, but that hadn't hit America yet. It just wasn't a commercially viable property."

About the unusual title Burroughs explained: "That was [from] a radio broadcast that came over when we were writing the book. There had been a circus fire, and I remember this phrase came through on the radio: 'And the hippos were boiled in their tanks!' So we used that as the title."

In his 1967 *Paris Review* interview, Jack Kerouac remembered the title's source this way: "It's called *And the Hippos Were Boiled in Their Tanks.* The hippos. Because Burroughs and I were sitting in a bar one night and we heard a newscaster saying '. . . and so the Egyptians attacked blah blah . . . and meanwhile there was a great fire in the zoo in London and the fire raced across the fields and the hippos were boiled in their tanks! Goodnight everyone!'

"That's Bill [Kerouac added], he noticed that. Because he notices them kind of things."

In yet another version, the fire was in the St. Louis zoo. But surely this is related to the Ringling Brothers and Barnum & Bailey Circus fire in Hartford, Connecticut, on July 6, 1944, known as "the day the clowns cried." There were nearly seven thousand people in the big tent when it was suddenly engulfed in flames; three minutes later the tent poles collapsed and the rest of the burning tent caved in. Six minutes after it all started there was nothing left but smoldering ashes. At least 165 men, women, and children died, and some five hundred more were injured, many trampled in the panic. It turned out that the tent's canvas had been waterproofed with a mixture of gasoline and paraffin —the opposite of a flame retardant.

The Hartford fire occurred within days of Burroughs's first visit to the 118th Street apartment to meet Kerouac, in late June or early July 1944. In Hartford, however, the horses, lions, elephants, and tigers were quickly led out of danger, and there were no hippos in Hartford to boil. A pygmy hippo reportedly died in the Cole Brothers Circus fire of 1940 in Rochester, Indiana, along with seventeen other exotic animals such as llamas and zebras; and in Cleveland, Ohio, a fire in the menagerie tent of the Ringling Brothers circus on August 4, 1942, had killed upwards of a hundred animals, two dozen of them shot down by police with high-powered rifles as the creatures fled in panic and horror, their fur ablaze. These horrific, absurd, grimly comic scenes were just the sort of thing that Burroughs found excruciatingly funny. Perhaps the boiling hippos was a running gag with him and it had been triggered again by news of the Hartford fire.

Others, such as Allen Ginsberg, remembered that the boiling-hippos line might have come from some early "cut-up" speech and radio-news experiments that their friend Jerry Newman used to make on his sound-recording devices. Newman was a Columbia student and jazz aficionado who, before magnetic tape recorders were available, got his hands on some portable disc-recording gear and took it to jam sessions and to the 52nd Street clubs; his rare 1940–41 recordings of Art Tatum are considered musical treasures.

In *Vanity of Duluoz*, his late-life novel as memoir, Kerouac described his collaboration with Burroughs in the winter of 1944–45.

Why, old Will in that time, he just awaited the next monstrous production from the pen of his young friend, me, and when I brought them in he pursed his lips in an attitude of amused inquiry and read. Having read what I offered up, he nodded his head and returned the production to the hands of the maker. Me, I sat there, perched on a stool somewhat near this man's feet, either in my room or in his apartment on Riverside Drive, in a conscious attitude of adoring expectation, and, finding my work returned to me with no more comment than a nod of the head, said, almost blushingly, "You've read it, what you think?"

The man Hubbard nodded his head, like a Buddha, having come to ghastly life from out of Nirvana what else was he s'posed to do? He joined his fingertips resignedly. Peering over the arch of his hands he answered, "Good, good."

"But what do you specifically think of it?"

"Why ..." pursing his lips and looking away toward a sympathetic and equally amused wall, "why, I don't specifically *think* of it. I just rather like it, is all."

The *Hippos* typescript was ready by early spring. In a letter of March 14, 1945, to his sister Caroline, Kerouac wrote, "[T]he book Burroughs and I wrote [...] is now in the hands of the publishing firm Simon & Schuster and they're reading it. What will happen I don't know. For the kind of book it is—a portrait of the 'lost' segment of our generation, hardboiled, honest, and sensationally real—it is good, but we don't know if those kinds of books are much in demand now, although after the war there will no doubt be a veritable rash of 'lost generation' books and ours in that field can't be beat."

Burroughs had raised the same question about which

literary styles would be fashionable and commercial; as we know, Simon & Schuster took a pass on the "sensationally real" *Hippos* manuscript, and it was rejected by a few other publishers. But Kerouac continued to rework the material: in summer 1945, on his own, he made a complete revision of the *Hippos* story, calling the result variously "The Phillip Tourian Story," or "Ryko/Tourian Story," or "I Wish I Were You." He also based the characters "Michael" and "Paul" on himself and Lucien Carr in *Orpheus Emerged,* another piece written around this time and published in 2005; this unfinished novella also features characters based on Ginsberg and Burroughs.

After two years in Elmira, Lucien Carr was released. He returned to New York to rebuild his life from the ground up, and he was in no mood to indulge his dear friend Jack in any romanticized versions of the tragedy that had ended his youth. He discouraged any further efforts to rewrite or resubmit the *Hippos* text or any similar treatments. Lucien's friends knew he wanted to put all that behind him, but it was too good a story to leave alone— and they were writers, or they soon would be.

In his letters to Kerouac and Ginsberg from Elmira, Carr had maintained his jaunty, what-me-worry? tone, but it was obvious to him and everyone else that he would not be returning to Columbia University. Soon after his release he went to work for United Press International, starting as a copyboy. He married Francesca von Hartz, started a family (three sons, Simon, the novelist Caleb, and Ethan), and in 1956 was promoted to night news editor at UPI.

That same year, Lawrence Ferlinghetti's City Lights Books published Allen Ginsberg's breakthrough poem "Howl," with its dedication to Lucien. But Carr had "enjoyed" more than enough public notoriety; he asked his old friend Allen to refrain from mentioning his name in future editions. The 1940s were now a closed chapter of Carr's life, or so he understandably hoped.

Burroughs didn't care one way or the other. By 1946 he was in deep trouble with drugs, his feet at the top of the down escalator that deposited him, five years later, within an inner ring of hell in Mexico City, when he recklessly but unintentionally killed his wife of those years, Joan Vollmer Burroughs, with a shot through the forehead in a drunken party stunt on September 6, 1951. He had been writing for two years at that point, but his subject was not Jack Kerouac or Lucien Carr; his subject was junk and junkies—in New York and Lexington, Kentucky, in east Texas and New Orleans,

Louisiana, and ultimately in Mexico City—in other words, himself and his junco partners.

Jack Kerouac's first published novel, *The Town and the City* (1950), was a small-town-to-big-city bildungs-roman like Balzac's *Lost Illusions* but told as a family saga, with aspects of Jack and his relatives recombined into the Martin family. The book does feature a much-changed version of the Carr–Kammerer story, with "Kenneth Wood" and "Waldo Meister" drawn from Carr and Kammerer, but with the facts changed enough so that Lucien Carr was not widely recognizable.

Yet *The Town and the City* had not tapped all of Kerouac's fascination with the story. In a letter to Carl Solomon from San Francisco on April 7, 1952—after Solomon had been made an editor at Ace Books by his uncle, Ace's owner A. A. Wyn—Jack spoke of the *Hippos* book, which he was willing for Ace to publish.

"There's no leeriness on my part concerning paper-cover books," Kerouac wrote. "[F]act of the matter is, Burroughs and I wrote a sensational 200-page novel about Lucien murder in 1945 that 'shocked' all pub-lishers in town and also agents . . . Allen remembers it . . . if you want it, go to my mother's house with Allen and find it in my maze of boxes and suitcases, it's in a manila envelope, entitled (I think) I WISH I WERE YOU, and is 'by Seward Lewis' (they being our respective middle names). Bill himself would approve of this move, we spent a year on it, Lucien was mad, wanted us to bury it under a floorboard (so don't tell Lucien now)."

Jack may have been embellishing the shock factor somewhat, but he was right about no one accepting *Hippos* for publication—including Ace Books in 1952. (And he still remembered those floorboards fifteen years later during *The Paris Review* interview.)

By 1959 the three cornerstone works of the Beats were published, and each of the three writers rapidly gained notoriety, readers, and sales. The Beat generation had tentatively received its name in John Clellon Holmes's 1952 novel *Go* (which also casts Carr and Kammerer in walk-on roles), but *Life* magazine's story in November 1959, "The Only Rebellion Around," was probably the dam burst of mainstream Beat awareness in America.

In 1959, as Gerald Nicosia points out in his essential biography *Memory Babe*, Kerouac was still making noises about reviving the *Hippos* story; he was stuck, halfway through his unfinished novel *Desolation Angels*. Indeed, he talked about it in front of Lucien and his wife Cessa: "terrifying her, and profoundly disturbing [Lucien] . . . Jack seemed to admire the killing as a heroic deed. Although at their behest he temporarily agreed not to do the book, he would keep bringing up the idea every few months, pushing Cessa to the brink of hysteria."

In 1967 Jack finally made good on his threat: he was writing *Vanity of Duluoz: An Adventurous Education 1935–46*, a book about his life before he went on the road with Neal Cassady, written as if told to his long-suffering third wife, Stella Sampas Kerouac. He hauled his old typescripts from 1945 out of the filing cabinet to reread for inspiration and reminders, and when *Vanity* was published in 1968 fully a fifth of the book was the story of "Claude de Maubris" (Lucien) and "Franz Mueller" (Kammerer). He also introduced the sublime "Wilson Holmes 'Will' Hubbard" (Burroughs) in language similar to what we find in *Hippos;* Kerouac's narrative process in *Vanity* also follows the *Hippos* scene structure fairly closely.

Kerouac's book was published just in time, because by 1968 the first Beat biographies were under way. Jane Kramer's *Allen Ginsberg in America* from that year was based on her recent series about Allen in *The New Yorker,* but she made no mention of Lucien Carr or David Kammerer; perhaps Allen simply refrained from talking about that story with her.

Next was Ann Charters's groundbreaking *Kerouac: A Biography* in 1973, and it reintroduced Carr and Kammerer to a world that had forgotten them—

whereas the UPI senior editor Lou Carr was well known and well liked. Charters, however (and Ginsberg used to complain about this in my presence), was obliged to remove from her last draft and replace with paraphrase every word she had quoted from the writings of Jack Kerouac, published or otherwise, because the Kerouac estate had an exclusive-access agreement with Aaron Latham, who was also working on a biography.

Latham's book was eventually completed but never published, perhaps because Charters's book was felt to have saturated the Kerouac-biography market for the time being. Meanwhile, important new biographies of Kerouac did come out in the 1970s, notably *Jack's Book* by Barry Gifford and Lawrence Lee, in 1978, and *Desolate Angel* by Dennis McNally in 1979.

The Latham project had a delayed effect that proved quite profound. Latham's agent was the venerable Sterling Lord, who was also Kerouac's agent since the early 1950s and, after Kerouac's death in October 1969, the estate's agent. Latham often wrote for *New York* magazine, and the late Clay Felker, its editor, agreed to publish Latham's first chapter. It was titled simply enough "The Columbia Murder that Gave Birth to the Beats," and it was published in April 1976, with a two-page graphic spread and, on the issue's cover, a reefer banner to the story inside. Latham's chapter was based directly on scenes and dialogue quoted liberally or paraphrased from *Vanity of Duluoz* and the unpublished *Hippos* typescript, as if both texts could be treated as literal, verbatim accounts. Lucien's intimacies with Ginsberg also made an unprecedented appearance in print.

The *New York* piece upset the applecart of Carr's life, and Lou was livid. Although he had worked with some of his friends at UPI for as long as thirty years, none of them had been aware of his adolescent homicide. He blamed Allen for talking about their sexual affairs too freely with Latham on tape; he felt that Allen had flouted the understanding of 1944, best summed up in *Vanity of Duluoz* when Claude mutters to the narrator (Jack), while both are in police custody, "Heterosexuality all the way down the line." Allen was unsure as to whether he had blabbed anything to Aaron Latham or not. Either way, he was all contrition and begged William to soothe Lucien's savage breast.

William felt quite indignant on Lucien's behalf, and with the help of his longtime copyright lawyer, Eugene H. Winick, he brought suit against Latham, Lord, and *New York* magazine for copyright infringement of Burrough's chapters the *Hippos* work, defamation of character, and invasion of privacy (meaning an unauthorized, endorsement-type use of one's name or likeness). Burroughs's suit was settled in the early

1980s for nominal damages and with no hard feelings; control of *Hippos* was thenceforth to be shared and exercised jointly. So now "the *Hippos* were locked in their drawer" —and thus matters stood for twenty years.

Burroughs moved from his New York "Bunker" to Lawrence, Kansas, at the end of 1981 and he lived and worked in Lawrence for sixteen more years, completing his Red Night Trilogy and creating a substantial body of visual art. When William Burroughs's time to make his journey to the Western Lands finally came, on August 2, 1997, I was with him; I had been privileged to live and work with William for twenty-three years.

Soon after my twenty-first birthday I had arrived in New York from Kansas to seek my destiny. Burroughs and the Beats had been my literary focus since my early teens; I had already met Ginsberg the year before and now, with Allen's encouragement, I met William, in mid-February 1974. William soon invited me to be his roommate in his big loft sublet at 452 Broadway. Very late one night that spring William and I were awakened by the street-door buzzer and I heard a cheerfully insolent voice bark over the intercom: "Bill! It's Lou Carr goddamn it, let me in." I did, and then we all sat up talking for an hour or two. My friendship with

Lucien began that night and grew over my years with William.

In fall 1999, as executor of the Burroughs estate, I took part in the Allen Ginsberg estate's auction at Sotheby's in New York. After the auction I went down to Washington, D.C., to visit Lou for a few days. There I affirmed my long-ago promise to Lucien: that, out of respect for his feelings, I would not allow publication of the Kerouac–Burroughs *Hippos* book in his lifetime.

I have also been gifted for many years with the friendship of John Sampas, executor of the Kerouac estate. John has been generous, thoughtful, and entertaining. He has also been consistently respectful of my promises to Lucien about *Hippos.*

They are all gone away now: Dave, Jack, Allen, Bill —and Lucien, too, three years ago, in 2005 . . . so here are your *Hippos*, ready at long last to come to the boil.

A few words about this book: the seasoned Beat reader will easily recognize the pseudonymous characters in *Hippos:* the real-life authors and narrators, Jack Kerouac ("Mike Ryko") and William Burroughs ("Will Dennison"); the tragic central figures Lucien Carr ("Phillip Tourian") and Dave Kammerer ("Ramsay Allen" or "Al"); Kerouac's girlfriend and first wife, Edie

Parker ("Janie"); Carr's girlfriend Celine Young ("Barbara 'Babs' Bennington"); and Carr's fellow freshman John Kingsland ("James Cathcart").

Scholars may also recognize some lesser-known historical persons on the fringes of the story: Lucien's parents, Russell Carr ("Mr. Tourian"/"Mr. Rogers") and Marion Carr ("Mrs. Tourian"); his wealthy uncle Godfrey S. Rockefeller ("Phillip's uncle" also); the future *New Yorker* writer Chandler Brossard, who lived at 48 Morton Street, where Kammerer lived, around the corner from Burroughs's apartment on Bedford Street (Brossard may be "Chris Rivers"); the longshoreman Neal Spollen ("Hugh Maddox"); a Barnard-linked lesbian circle, with the butch Ruth Louise McMahon ("Agnes O'Rourke") and the femme undergrads Donna Leonard ("Della") and Teresa Willard ("Bunny"?); Kammerer's friend Patricia Goode Harrison and her then-husband Thomas F. Healy, an Irish writer ("Jane Bole and Tom Sullivan," possibly); and the young gangster whom only Dennison knows—based on one "Hoagy" Norman, or Norton ("Danny Borman").

And of course Joe Gould, the real-life "Professor Sea Gull"—as he was dubbed in a widely read 1942 profile by Joseph Mitchell in *The New Yorker*—appears here under his own name. Verbose, alcoholic, middle-aged, a patrician *dans la boue* fallen from a family tree with roots in pre-Revolutionary Boston, Gould was an authentic Village eccentric. Just as portrayed in *Hippos,* he passed his time at the Minetta Tavern, working (he said) on his vast literary masterpiece, *An Oral History of Our Time*—and, as Burroughs recalled, doing his "seagull act" for drinks. But "Joe Gould's Secret," which Mitchell revealed in his 1964 follow-up, was that the endlessly scribbled manuscript of the *Oral History* had never existed.

In 2000 *Joe Gould's Secret* was made into a film, directed by Stanley Tucci and starring Ian Holm as Gould. It is a beautifully realized visual re-creation of exactly the place and time—Greenwich Village in the mid-1940s—when this *Hippos* story takes place, and thus the reader might do well to screen the movie to help in reimagining these settings, so distant now in time.

In my editing, I have not aspired to the kind of meticulous textual work that the eminent Burroughs scholar Oliver Harris has already brought to his definitive versions of Burroughs's early works *Junky* (1953) and *The Yage Letters* (1963). Rather, I have endeavored to present these writings according to the authors' own intentions, insofar as those can be discerned.

We do know that Kerouac and Burroughs entrusted this selfsame typescript, entire, to their agent in spring

1945, for submission to publishers such as Simon & Schuster and Random House. This fact alone confirms to me that, if *Hippos* had been contracted for publication then, they very likely would have acquiesced in some modest editorial suggestions as to organization and orthography—especially since they were writing explicitly for a genre-fiction market, not for the avant-garde reader.

I have largely avoided making silent changes, though I have made a few. Commas were added only when they seemed quite necessary, and some solecisms have even been retained, as being characteristic of the authors' composition style. Jack Kerouac evidently typed up this entire manuscript just as it is preserved, with no missing pages; he was a good speller and handy with punctuation. My greatest liberty was taken in adding or changing paragraph breaks, to enhance readability or the almost cinematic scenarization—again, as seems appropriate to the work's literary genre.

Before I close, below, a note about the text: it was transcribed from archival photocopies of the typescripts by my friend and colleague Tom King, whom I am pleased to thank for his painstaking help. I want to thank also my friends Thomas Peschio, John Curry, and James M. Smith for manifold favors and encouragements; scholars Gerald Nicosia, Oliver Harris, Dave

Moore, and Bill Morgan for suggestions and error res-
cues; my editor Jamison Stoltz for guidance timely prof-
fered; Lucien's companion Kathleen Silvassy for their
hospitality to me, years ago; my old friend Gene Winick
for a lifetime of help to William and his legacy, and
likewise the Kerouac estate's agent Sterling Lord for
his six decades' nurturance of Jack's legacy (and his
magnanimity around that bygone lawsuit thirty years
ago); my friend and colleague John Sampas, for his even
keel and Burroughsian wit; my agents Andrew Wylie
and Jeff Posternak, for years of faith in me, through
my vicissitudes; my cherished and dear friend Ira Silver-
berg for all the above and much more; but most of all
my beloved mother, Selda Paulk Grauerholz, who
passed away on March 13, 2008, still asking me did I
have the *Hippos* done yet!—her, I thank for everything,
always, and wish I could tell her so again.

Lou Carr became a consummate and dedicated news-
man. He was promoted to head of UPI's news desk in
the 1970s, and when United Press relocated to Washington, D.C., in 1983 he moved there from New York.
Lucien remained with the agency forty-seven years,
until his retirement in 1993 at age sixty-eight. He died,
aged seventy-nine, on January 28, 2005.

At a tribute event at the National Press Club in Washington, D.C., on March 4, 2005, more than 160 of Lucien Carr's fellow journalists gathered to eulogize him. As the *Times* of London reported in its obituary: "A history of the [United Press] company, *Unipress* (2003), said of Carr that he was: 'the soul of the news service. The tall, slim graduate of the "Beat Generation" rewrote, repaired, recast and revived more big stories on UPI's main newspaper circuit, the *A-wire*, than anyone before or after him.' He inspired much admiration and affection from colleagues."

"The murder that gave birth to the Beats" has become an oft-told tale, but it was not the death of Kammerer that rocked the cradle of the Beats; it was the intellectual and sexual life force of teenaged Lucien Carr, whom Kammerer himself had raised from puberty on a rich diet of poetic excess—the divine afflatus of Baudelaire; the *actes gratuits* of Gide; and the passionate entwinement of Verlaine and Rimbaud. And then Dave and Lucien fell into madness, enacting those doomed roles in their own lives.

In *Hippos,* Jack and Bill portrayed a tragic case of mentorship gone wrong and the natural cruelty of youth. However, the plot difficulty with *Hippos* was always that Kammerer's death was not the end of a story but the beginning of one. With Kammerer dead and Carr locked up, three remained: Burroughs, Kerouac, and Ginsberg . . . and although none of them would see their work published for another decade after David died, they were the ones destined for recognition, literary and otherwise.

Lucien Carr's limelight moment as the insouciant young cynosure of the Beats—the lucent, charismatic Claude de Maubris, their sacrificial celebrant, cheering them on to *"Plonger au fond du gouffre / Enfer ou Ciel, qu'importe?"*—that halcyon time ended many years ago, one hot summer night in wartime when Lucien took, or accepted, the life of his mentor and soft touch, his stalker and plaything, his creator and destroyer, David Eames Kammerer.

—James W. Grauerholz
June 2008